D1531141

Acknowledgements:
To Heather for her help.
Contains artwork by Alexandre Cabanel

Camille Oster - Author
http://www.facebook.com/pages/Camille-Oster/489718877729579
Camille.osternz@gmail.com

An Absent Wife

By Camille Oster

Chapter 1

St James Square, Mayfair, London, 1871

"IT SEEMS MY WIFE IS DEAD," Lord Lysander Warburton said and folded the crisp note sent from the Colonial Office. He returned the note to the silver tray placed by one of the club's butlers on the shined mahogany table next to his chair in the quiet reading room.

Lysander's dearest friend, Harry, looked up from his paper and sniffed. "Good," he said. "Finally, the harlot is good enough to do something right."

"Careful, Harry," Lysander warned without any discernible sting in his voice. "She is my wife."

"Was, Lysander. No more. And good riddance to her."

Lysander considered the news. He couldn't remember exactly the last time he'd seen his wife. It must have been at his nephew's christening two years ago. He turned over the implications of her death in his head.

He'd always said his marriage was the worst thing that ever happened to him—even before the tart had run off with some useless lieutenant. Lysander couldn't remember his name. That wasn't strictly true, his name was Samson Ellingwood—a man of little consequence—but Lysander liked to think that he couldn't remember the man's name. He'd bristled at her lack of propriety, if anything—she could have carried on discreetly with her...friend, as is expected, but instead, she had to resort to dramatics and run off like some witless character in an eighteenth-century tragedy.

"Cholera apparently," Lysander stated quietly after a long silence.

"Nasty way to go," Harry said absently. "They would have burnt the body. Never mind, that is a shackle you can do without."

Lysander wasn't as convinced as his friend of the benefits of this turn of events as he was now fair game for all the unmarried women in London—not to mention his mistress, Evie, who would likely develop strange and trying ideas. He hated dramatics and hysterics, and he would likely be subjected to both in short order.

"It's a damned nuisance actually," Lysander admitted. It really was; he'd been plodding along quite happily living his life in London, while his wife occupied the Devon country house—a situation that had gone on for six years until her desertion.

He tried searching his feelings, but had trouble discerning what they were. He'd hated her from the start— the bride who had been forced on him at the tender age of twenty-three. He'd ignored her completely throughout the engagement, which in fact turned out to be almost as long as their marriage.

Over the years, his hatred had turned into indifference and he'd rarely given his marriage much thought until she'd run off with that ridiculous man, which had proved highly embarrassing as the news had spread across London. He hadn't expected it and there had been nothing he could do against the malicious gossip. There had been rumors of a pending divorce, but they had never discussed it—not that he'd had the opportunity to, but he could have had someone track her down if he'd needed to. Obviously, he'd considered the idea of divorcing her, but the concept itself was unseemly and he'd seen no real reason or benefit from it. While a divorce would make a statement to the gossips and such, it wouldn't actually improve his life, so he'd seen no rush; he only would have made himself a target for the cloying society mothers—a position he was now placed in anyway. No matter what the girl did, she was a nuisance.

Lysander stayed at the club and returned home shortly after nine in the evening. Normally, he would go to his mistress' house, but he wasn't disposed to. He supposed he'd pay some reverence to his late wife for the evening—not that she deserved it.

Arriving home and withdrawing to the comfortable chair in his study, he considered the abject failure that had been his marriage. His wedding band clinked slightly against the crystal whiskey glass as he picked it up. He'd worn it because it was his duty to—a duty he'd adhered to for the sake of propriety. She had always been sufficiently provided for; he'd given her requests due consideration when she'd written to him, and he'd never denied her anything reasonable or anything due to her position or status.

Adele Fowler, had been her name before he'd been forced to give her his, in an act to save the estate and family from ruination.

*

"I'm not marrying that girl," Lysander shouted after he'd burst into his father's study at the Mayfair house. He'd just heard the news from his mother that he was to marry the daughter of the disastrous family his father had invited to dinner the previous week. "Have you lost your mind?"

"I haven't lost my mind. There is nothing wrong with the girl. She's pretty enough."

"Her father's in trade. His name is Fowler for God's sake—could there be anything more common. Five hundred years of tradition and you want me to throw it all away on practically a ... heathen."

"Don't be so melodramatic. She's a lovely girl. Her manners were impeccable."

7

"And you wish to spend every future Christmas with that plow-horse of a father? I can't believe you have done this—I won't agree."

"You know very well why I have done this," his father roared. "You think this house keeps on nothing? You think the country estate keeps on nothing? We must replace the roof."

"And you are to sell me like livestock for a new roof?"

"Make no mistake; you are marrying this girl to save the honor and continuation of this family. The Fowlers have more money than the Queen and we are requisitioning it. You will marry the girl and you will smile while you're doing it." His father's hard side came out as he delivered his demand. It wasn't often that it did, but it was beyond doubt that he was serious. Lysander knew he would be disinherited if he didn't.

"My interests lie elsewhere," Lysander finally said. "There is a girl—"

"Not anymore," his father cut in. "This is your duty, Lysander—one you will have to perform and that is just the way it is. There is no point fighting it. Our family needs this money or we will slide into genteel poverty like the Havishworths, losing all of our property with nothing to our names other than a title. Is that the future you foresee for us? I don't care if this annoys you Lysander; you will do it."

Lysander clenched his fists tighter before storming out of the room. He left the house and didn't return for ten days. His rebelliousness had stayed until he had run out of money and he had to return home, knowing full well that the speech his father would give him when he turned up in his study asking for more money.

*

Lysander sniffed at the memory of the awful conversation with his now late father before taking another swig of his drink. He listened to the quiet of the house before his thoughts wandered back to the past. Cassandra had been the name of the girl he'd wanted to marry. She was smart

8

and sassy, with a wicked sense of humor. She'd been the one amongst all his acquaintances who everyone had adored, but she had definitely treated Lysander with more consideration than the rest.

She was still the same now—the life of the party—but she was married to Lord Alterstrong, who she affectionately called a 'brute of a man.' Cassandra would always ask where he kept that elusive wife of his, but Lysander had never relented and brought his wife with him to any of his social occasions. The only time he saw Adele was at family functions. She wasn't exactly the uncouth creature he'd expected; her manners were impeccable, which only made her even more dull in his eyes. She'd developed a friendship with his aunt of all people and he knew they wrote to each other and they spent time together whenever they were in the same vicinity.

Adele was just ... boring. Everything about her was dull. She was pretty enough, but she had no sass or wit. She'd never succeeded in making him laugh. She was just there and he'd had no trouble forgetting her, even when she was present.

Her desertion had come as a true surprise. At first, he'd dismissed it as absurd teasing when he'd heard through a letter from one of the neighbors, but as more news came from the staff at the country house, it had turned out to be true—she'd run off with some military man who'd been stationed in the district. Truthfully, Lysander had been more annoyed than hurt. It was beyond reason that he should be cuckolded by his mouse of a wife. It was an absurd notion and he would have laughed heartily if it had happened to someone else.

All in all, he hadn't been a great husband. His anger at her being forced on him had marred any potential affection he could have developed for her and time only cemented the chasm between them. He wasn't sure what kind of marriage she had expected going into this; he'd no idea what her expectations were in regards to anything, but she got to live in a fine country house and she'd been respected in Devon county. She'd been a lady and had been referred to as such, any insult to her status would have been an insult to his and the good people of Devon wouldn't have dared.

But she'd given it all up to be a consort of a lowly Lieutenant, an action he could neither understand nor condone, but she'd done it—rejected everything he offered: the security, the status and respect, to cavort with a man who could offer her nothing but social subjugation and notoriety. He knew her well enough to know that notoriety was not what she sought. She'd been a paragon of respectability, bending on none of the required etiquette and he had silently ridiculed her for it.

It had never been a success of a marriage and he wasn't sure it could ever have been. They were too dissimilar, having come from completely different backgrounds. How could it have been that they could have made a success of a marriage he didn't want? It was the fault of their fathers, who'd sought gains beyond the happiness of their children. They had both paid for their greed by forgoing the happiness of their children. But then the Fowlers' wealth had been absorbed into the family, making them a formidable family again. There was no doubt it was her wealth that had done it. He'd always believed that her gain in status and rise in society had been a good bargain in her eyes; it wasn't until her desertion that he'd come to realize that maybe it was not.

Harry was right in that her body would have been burnt as was the custom with cholera victims. There was no body for him to collect, but he still felt as if he had to go and collect her things. In line with her propensity for being a

10

nuisance, he had to go all the way to India to do it. That is where they'd run off to. Lieutenant Ellingwood had taken on a lowly commission far away from England, as was required by military men who took on inappropriate consorts.

Not only did it confound him that a man would so depress his own prospects for a woman—his mousy wife no less—but it also irked him. Something about the whole thing sat very badly with him.

With a sigh, he concluded that he must travel to India to bring her possessions back to England. He hadn't been a good husband, but he would do this for her and not leave her forgotten and ignored in death in some far-off country. He owed the Fowlers that much. It would be a long, arduous voyage, but he hoped that if he did this, he would be comfortable putting this whole debacle behind him.

Chapter 2

"YOU STUPID, STUPID MAN," came the rather unexpected reaction from his aunt Isobel when he went around to tell her the news of Adele's demise. The distressed woman with brown hair like his confronted him.

"I really can't see how you can lay the blame of this on me," he defended himself as he stood in his aunt's sumptuous parlor.

"You let her run off with that man—to India of all places—a place with every tropical disease under the sun. It was only a matter of time before she caught something." Isobel's voice faded and she brought her hand to her forehead in a clear sign of distress. Truthfully, Isobel's reaction annoyed him. She'd always insisted on being Adele's champion—even after everything the stupid girl had done. If anyone was responsible for Adele's death, it was Adele and her lover. He certainly hadn't sent her traipsing off across the world to conduct an illicit affair.

"I most certainly did not." He hadn't expected such a strong reaction from his aunt who was pacing up and down in front of the window, failing to see why his aunt would blame this on him. It only reiterated how illogical women were, or else his aunt hadn't entirely grasped the situation. Perhaps senility was setting in. She was a bit young for senility, but she could be one of the unlucky few who were afflicted early in life. He vowed that he would have to keep a closer eye on his aunt in case that was true.

"Men!" she said with unguarded anger.

"I am going to go there and collect her things."

This seemed to calm his aunt and she nodded. "You have informed her family?"

"I have. I went around and saw her cousin." It had been an unpleasant task, but luckily the relationship between Adele and her older male cousin hadn't been close and the news was received as unfortunate, but not overly distressing. Lysander was grateful that Adele's parents were not alive to hear such sad news, but he supposed they were all together now. He wasn't entirely sure he believed that, but it was nice to think it was true.

"When are you leaving?"

"Tomorrow."

His aunt nodded again.

"I am traveling through the Suez," he said. His aunt turned away, giving him her back. He had upset her again. "I need to make some preparations."

Isobel finally turned back to him and her face softened. "Be safe. Don't take any risks."

"I am only going to India; I'm not invading a country."

"All the same, be careful. It is India; it has dangers beyond what we know here. You must come back in one piece or you will break my heart."

"Yes, Aunt," he said, slightly embarrassed that she sometimes had a tendency to treat him like a boy. He had accepted a certain lack of constancy in her character—her emotions seemed to sway her into illogical responses. Giving his aunt a kiss, he escaped out of her house. It was always difficult dealing with his aunt, but he knew she cared for him and ultimately wanted what was best for him—even if she had strange ways of showing it sometimes—ways he didn't understand.

That was the last requirement. He'd already told Evie, who insisted on coming with him, but he had refused her offer. While he understood that Evie would like for them to travel together—doing so for the purpose of collecting his late wife's belongings was inappropriate. Perhaps when he came back, he would take her somewhere and they could move past the whole strain of this debacle.

*

Lysander boarded the train to Dover at London Bridge, where he ran into Nigel Tunbridge, whose company he could keep all the way to Paris, where he would change trains to continue to Venice. His private compartment was comfortable when he wanted solitude to watch the scenery go by. Nigel, with his pervasive interest in birds, could be trying company as he explained the habits and destinations of every flying thing they saw out the window.

Lysander wondered if this was the way that his wife had come when she ran off with her friend—likely having an intimate time with her new lover. Perhaps he should have brought Evie after all, considering the reverence Adele had shown to her obligations when she'd traveled. But he was a better man and would show appropriate behavior where it was due.

He recalled their wedding, where he'd been an angry and sullen young man. He hadn't been rude to the girl, whose eyes had been large with anxiety. She'd barely spoken loud enough for the Vicar to hear her answers and her hand had been cold too, on that late October morning when they'd said their oaths in the parish church in Devon. Her dress was elegant, but it didn't take due consideration to the weather and she looked pale and drawn with cold.

Changing trains in Paris occurred without much trouble and he got to say goodbye to Tunbridge on the platform. The porters organized the moving of his belongings and he only had to wait half an hour in Paris before he was on his way to Venice. He hadn't been back to Venice since his youth and didn't entirely appreciate the reminders of that carefree time. It had been a time before he had known that Adele would be forced on his life.

Lysander whiled away the hours by reading, playing cards and engaging with the people who were traveling to Venice. The first-class compartment included respectable people of mostly English and French origin, and it was noteworthy how easily connections could be drawn between the people on the train, even the French. Everyone knew someone who knew someone. It wasn't a large world they inhabited, he conceded.

He'd made a few new acquaintances by the time he had to board the ship set for India. Lysander hadn't done a great deal of sailing—only the short trips between Dover and Calais—so a longer journey was something new. He watched as Venice with all its history sail past as they left on the evening tide.

The ship wasn't large, requiring appropriate dimensions for the Suez Canal imposed restrictions on the ships that could pass through, but it was a well-appointed ship, meant for travel by people of consequence. A number of high-ranking British Military men were on board—a few whom he knew through social circles.

He relaxed as they sailed through the blue waters of the Mediterranean, marveling at the different light and colors this far south. Luckily it wasn't summer, so excessive heat didn't burden him, but it did get warmer the closer they got to the Suez, where beasts pulled the ship slowly along the canal. Egyptian men with their tanned faces and white robes worked along the edges of the canal, guiding the beasts and selling all manners of things. The local men gathering to force the ship around some irregularity in the wall of the newly finished canal.

"Marvellous achievement this," a General Hastings said. "May be the best feat of engineering in the history of the world."

"It certainly cuts down on the arduousness of the journey to India," Lysander responded. "For which I am grateful."

"Certainly does. Much more civilized than spending six months sailing around the Horn, constantly reacquainting yourself with the contents of your stomach. A man loses his bulk in that manner; although I must say, there are a few who would actually be better off for it."

Lysander liked General Hastings—a no-nonsense man, who was set to relieve another General in Madras. "I have never had the misfortune of experiencing that route."

"And we will concede that we are now living in a better age."

"Indeed."

"What brings you to India?" the General asked.

Lysander looked away considering what to say. It would only prove embarrassing if he admitted he was traveling to collect the things of his inconstant wife. "Business."

"Well, here's to fruitful business," the General said, holding up his glass. "What are you drinking?"

"Claret."

"Best start acquiring a taste for gin; it is necessary with the malaria that's constantly hanging about. Should start building up your resistance now."

"Of course," Lysander said. He'd forgotten about the malaria and placed an order with one of the servers, to be delivered an ample glass of gin and tonic—not a drink he normally chose, but the taste was not unpleasant. It was actually refreshing in the heat.

"Your wife will not miss you on such a long journey?"

"I dare say not."

"It is good to get away from them at times. My wife chides me every time, but she knew I was a military man when she married me. Odd creatures, women."

Lysander didn't argue.

*

Arriving in Bombay was challenging. If it hadn't been for his weariness of seeing nothing but ocean, he may well have turned back. As soon as he got off the ship, his senses were assaulted by everything at once. There were people yelling at him in languages he didn't understand. The sun was bright and the heat beating down on his head as he moved away from the cool sea breezes and the shade of the ship's decks. He hadn't actually been aware that heat could be this oppressive. His clothes stuck to every part of his body and he felt he couldn't draw breath properly.

Two men grabbed his trunk when the ship's porters placed it on the docks. Lysander didn't engage the men and he didn't entirely trust them, but they had his trunk and were waiting for him to move, following behind when he finally did move after a few moments trying to orientate himself.

He saw General Hastings across the crowded dock, who gave a wave before getting into an open carriage that clearly belonged to the military. Lysander felt envious that there was a greeting party for the General when he—as a private person—was left to find a way on his own. Still, the General's carriage struggled to get through the crowd.

Lysander walked into the port's administrative building, which looked elegant, but the crowd inside provided no reprieve. A sea of white-covered bodies, some of them not entirely covered, Lysander noted. He finally found a European man wearing trousers and a vest.

"Good morning, I am Lord Warburton and I need to take the train to Calcutta." Someone pushed him from behind as he spoke and he almost crashed into the man he was speaking to. Annoyance gripped him, at the rudeness and lack of consideration.

"Pleasure, my Lord. Francis Sallerser, East India Company. At your service. You will have to make your way to the train station. A rickshaw would be best. Just pick one outside; they will accept any coin." He pointed to the other side of the building and Lysander groaned when he realized he had to make his way across the crowd again.

"It is always like this?"

"Welcome to India," the man said with a beaming grin. "It gets worse. Good luck." The man patted him on the shoulder before his attention was drawn away and he shouted something at a man in what Lysander assumed was the local language.

Lysander turned to the men standing behind him. "Rickshaw," he said and they blinked for a moment before turning to eye each other, then turning and leading the way—roughly forcing their way through the crowd. These men had no qualms about pushing their way through the crush and Lysander congratulated himself on his own inventiveness in letting these local men navigate the throng.

They picked a rickshaw for him and had his trunk loaded at the back of the contraption on which Lysander had to awkwardly climb up after paying his porters a few coins. He grabbed onto the sides as he felt as if he was falling as the man picked up the poles in front and started pulling it along, struggling with the weight. Lysander wasn't sure this would work, but the man got the thing going and pulled them out of the covered driveway of the port building.

It didn't take long for Lysander to understand the meaning of the East India Company's man when he said that things got worse. The street was too narrow for the traffic and every inch of it was covered by a body, a cart or a rickshaw. The rickshaws were definitely more nimble and Lysander tried not to jump every time a collision seemed narrowly avoided, much to his surprise.

The heat of the sun still beat on him and he was further accosted by the bright colors everywhere, and smells he couldn't even describe. Women wore all manners of bright colors and there were colors upon colors everywhere he looked. There was no escape from the strange odors and they undulated from one pungent form to another, while the noise pounded his ears. He couldn't take it all in. Yet again, he considered returning to the ship where things were calm and normal. This was utter madness.

Another near miss with a cart made his heart twist as he held onto the sides so his fingers were white. He had no idea where he was or where he was going. This man struggling with his rickshaw through the crowd could be taking him anywhere. In the end, he just had to close his eyes to all the things that were coming at him.

It took a long time, but he finally arrived at a rail station. It was just as crowded as every other part of this place. He decided that the best thing for him to do was to focus on his immediate needs—getting his trunk down and into the building. Again, men appeared unasked and did it for him. He paid the rickshaw driver, having no idea how much his services were worth, but he seemed happy with the money he received and pulled his contraption away.

Lysander had no idea where to go, but just followed the men carrying his trunk. They led him to an Indian man dressed in European garb, who looked up from a desk, where he was writing with a brass stylus into a large book. Standing up, he nodded.

"I need to go to Calcutta," Lysander said, trying to hide his exasperation.

"There is a mail train that leaves in a few hours," the man said in perfect English to Lysander's surprise. "I will see if there are any first-class compartments available. I am assuming you wish to travel first class."

"Naturally."

"Can I suggest that you wait in the lounge in the meantime?" the man said, indicating to a set of marble stairs leading to the second story. "I will let you know if a compartment is available. You can leave your trunk here; I will see to it." Lysander thanked the man while praying that a greater power would be merciful and let him have a compartment. He didn't want to stay a night in this city, or longer depending on the next run of the mail train.

Following the stairs up, he was greeted by a spacious room with high ceilings and large blades moving around to encourage the circulation of air. Lysander sighed at the mere absence of people and noise. There were tables and chairs along one side where large windows lined the wall. A large bar lay against the back wall and a uniformed man with white gloves welcoming him, urging him to take a seat.

There were gentlemen and ladies sitting at some of the tables and Lysander sat down at a vacant table as the server took his order of gin and tonic. When he sat down, he could see nothing but blue sky and the calming greenery that had been installed in this room. Finally seated, he started to relax for the first time in hours. The tension in his shoulders wouldn't give, but he felt his mind relax somewhat. A large glass with a slice of lemon floating in its contents had appeared on his table when he opened his eyes again.

This might be heaven, he thought as he took a sip of the refreshing liquid in the cool, calm and quiet space. There was nothing but gentle chatter from the other parties further down the room. This he could manage.

Time had likely passed when he felt ready to think about his situation. Looking around the building, he noted its recent construction. He had read that the train service he was to board had only started a few months earlier. The world was reforming itself and he was watching the cusp of it. The old ways were abandoned and the new were forming, even along the breadth of the empire. He was seeing first-hand some spectacular achievements, bringing in the new world and he was quite excited about it. The newness of everything was provocative and intriguing, and he was living witness to an evolution. The Underground Railway had just been completed and extended in London. It seemed as though the whole city was under construction, transitioning into the new world. He felt pride in his own people and the achievements they had made. Their influence extended all over the world, as had the enthusiasm for improvement and progress. He knew that while the things he was experiencing were overwhelming, he would be glad he had seen them, in hindsight.

A man came and told him that his travel had been organized and he would be collected when the time was near. He appreciated the clear efficiency of the organization in the midst of the chaos outside this little tranquil haven.

When it was time to leave, he was escorted to his compartment. The platform was utter chaos, but as soon as he stepped into the first-class carriage of the train and sat down in his allocated compartment, he was encased in a little bubble of serene calm and luxury. The heat was still pervasive and he hoped that the movement of the train would generate a bit of a draft, or he would swelter before he ever reached Calcutta.

Sitting patiently, he watched the madness outside his window until he heard the whistle and felt the steam engine strain as it slowly pulled them away, providing him with a view of the city. The perception of utter chaos didn't desist until they left the city and they were traveling through the open countryside, which was beautiful and exotic—nothing like the English countryside. Buffalos were used to plow fields. He even saw the odd camel along the way as they passed small mud-brick villages. The color and the light were completely different as well, softer and more golden.

The food was excellent, which pleased him and he gave into his exhaustion as soon as dusk set in and had the train butler prepare his compartment for the night as soon as his supper was cleared away. The only unfortunate thing was the lack of a dining cart, which meant that this service had limited options for socializing or even moving about the train.

He grew used to the constant movement of the train, but the stops woke him. The noise of people loading mail and goods on and off the train throughout the night interrupted his sleep, but those same stops gave him a few moments to walk around and smoke once day had broken. It was a good chance to meet and talk to the other passengers in the first-class carriage. The stations away from the cities weren't as crowded and it was pleasant to take a turn around the platform.

Lysander wasn't surprised by the confusion of Calcutta when he arrived, being no different from Bombay, maybe even warmer, but he wasn't sure. He had himself transported to the offices of the Colonial Office to meet the man, a Mr. Parsons, who had initially sent him the telegraph informing him of his wife's death.

Greeting the man, a Mr. Parsons informed him that sadly her remains had been incinerated and Lysander confirmed he had expected it.

"Her effects are still being held at the hotel she was staying at, awaiting instructions from her family."

"I have come to collect them."

"Of course," Mr. Parsons said somberly. "I will run you over there."

They were met outside by a horse-drawn carriage carrying the British Royal seal. It was a more stable ride than the rickshaws, but also more cumbersome on the narrow streets.

It was clear that Mr. Parsons was uncomfortable with the task of assisting him in retrieving his wife's effects from the place where she had been living with her lover. The whole concept made him feel uncomfortable as well, if more for the unspoken things.

They arrived at the hotel and it was a large structure with a sizeable stairway leading up to the main lobby. The floor was tiled black and white in the open and cool space of the lobby, where a large dark wood desk was manned by a British man who Mr. Parsons seemed to be familiar with. They spoke quietly amongst themselves before the man smiled at Lysander.

"You have my deepest condolences, My Lord. She was a lovely woman and she deserved a better fate than dying of cholera. It was not an easy death, but she had the best medical treatment available—the Surgeon General's office saw to her directly, but sadly they were unable to save her. Where would you like to send her things?" he asked discreetly.

"To my room if you have one available." It looked like a nice enough place and he decided he would much prefer to stay here than fight his way through the streets again. The restaurant over to the left looked inviting, as did the bar.

Waiting while the room was prepared, he said goodbye to Mr. Parson who had to return to his duties after offering his services for anything further he required.

Lysander was shown to a room on the second story—a large, spacious room with dark wooden floors and white walls. Large slatted shutters kept the sun out while letting air circulate. The shutters opened onto a large, lush garden below. His wife's lover hadn't chosen a bad hotel, he noted. This would be a good place for lovers, a tranquil reprieve in the chaos of India. He wondered if her room had been like his and what they did here other than... Sharply dismissing the thought, he turned to the large canopied bed covered with a gauzy looking material meant to keep out the mosquitos at night. An uninvited image of his wife riding a man flashed into his head before a knock on the door made it dissipate like mist. Opening the door revealed the proprietor holding a box, which Lysander guessed was the remains of his wife's life. The man carried two boxes inside, placing them on a table.

"What should I do with Mr. Ellingwood's effects?" the man said quietly, not much louder than a whisper.

Lysander considered it for a moment, then straightened his spine. "Bring them here. I will take them back and have them forwarded to his family." He felt the sting of having to deal with her lover's issues as well, but he was a gentleman and he would see to a fellow Englishman's needs in a foreign country on behalf of his family—irrespective of any personal injuries that person would have caused him.

Another box was delivered a short time later by a young Indian boy.

Lysander ignored the boxes for the rest of the day. He had dinner, drank in the garden with the other guests and slept until dawn when the heat returned, robbing him of further sleep. Lying in bed, he considered how long he would stay. He wasn't ready to start heading back as he hadn't even begun to recover from his trip here.

There was still something very uncomfortable about being in this place where his wife had been, and had claimed a life away from the one he provided. He still didn't understand what it was that had made her do it; it was an illogical decision as this man she was with could truly offer her very little. He wondered about the man who had urged a woman to give up her respectability, her station and her security, eyeing the box with Ellingwood written on one side. His pride battled with his curiosity, but he left the box alone until the time he returned from breakfast down in the restaurant. Finally opening the box, he found the typical things—clothing, toiletries, his watch engraved with a message of devotion for someone named Charles Ellingwood. There was nothing out of the ordinary amongst his possessions. Looking amongst the man's possessions, he wondered if his wife had given him anything here. He didn't know her well enough to hazard a guess.

He then moved to his wife's box. Its contents were roughly the same, but everything was finer in nature—silks, brushes and a small bottle of French perfume. Opening it, he tried to place the scent, but it didn't register as familiar to him. He wondered if he should know his wife's perfume. It seemed strange that he was married to this woman and didn't know the scent she preferred.

There was no journal and he was relieved. He didn't want to know her thoughts or what she'd been thinking when she'd deserted her home and her husband, or the feelings she'd had for the man she'd shared a room with, likely very similar to this one.

*

He received a message a few days later informing him that Mr. Parson was in the lobby, and he went downstairs to meet the man, who again gave him the Colonial Office's deepest condolences for his loss. Mr. Parsons had been charged with delivering an invitation to dine with the Viceroy at the end of the week.

Lysander graciously accepted the invitation, saying that it would be an honor and a delight.

"Mr. Parsons, there is one thing I would like to ask of you," Lysander said before Mr. Parsons left. "I would like to see where my wife and... Mr. Ellingwood's remains are."

"Of course," Mr. Parsons said. "You understand there will be no sign of them." Lysander nodded and Mr. Parsons went to speak to the manager.

They rode out into the madness of the city in Mr. Parsons' carriage. Lysander couldn't orientate himself in this city at all, but Mr. Parsons seemed to know where he was going and they arrived along a muddy looking river, where uneven stairs went down to terraces by the water.

"This is where ..." Mr. Parsons said uncomfortably, "where cadavers are burnt and disposed of. The Indians spread the ashes in the river. It is a great honor in their religion. We don't usually follow this custom with British citizens, but in the case of infectious disease, it is the best thing."

The various confronting smells gave way to another. It wasn't a smell he knew well, but he knew without a doubt what it was. A pyre was burning not far away from where they were standing. Lysander pulled out his handkerchief and covered his nose, but it did nothing to deter the pervasive stink.

"This is where she...?"

"Yes," Mr. Parsons said. "Unfortunately, there was no one from our office here at the time. Due to the nature of her illness ..." he drifted off. "The outbreak has abated, but we do get them coming through from time to time. Damned unlucky in this case." Mr. Parsons called to someone, speaking the local language. A man came forward, wearing nothing other than a cloth wrapped around his private area and another on his head. "This is the man who saw to the victims from the hotel."

The man spoke animatedly, moving his head oddly sideways as he did so, turning his palm over as he spoke.

"He said the man's ashes were spread in the river," Mr. Parsons conveyed.

Lysander sighed at the lack of a proper Christian ritual. "Wait, what about the woman?"

Mr. Parsons spoke to the man who started shaking his head again. They spoke animatedly between them as Lysander watched. Mr. Parsons finally turned to him and opened his mouth, seemingly trying to formulate his words. Lysander narrowed his eyes knowing that something uncomfortable was about to come. He didn't want to hear about something unfortunate, or worse, something uncondonable happening to his wife's body.

"He says…" the man blustered and Lysander stared at him intently. "He says… there was only one body—a man."

"What of the woman?" Lysander said through clenched teeth.

Mr. Parsons turned to the man and spoke rapidly before turning back.

"The only woman he saw was alive; she was standing about where you are. She had a yellow dress and she had hair like—" Mr. Parsons said something he couldn't understand. "It is a grain that is a light brown color."

"Is my wife dead or not?" Lysander said icily.

"I think I had better … I need to speak to some people. If you would bear with me for a moment."

Chapter 3

ADELE LOOKED AROUND THE classroom where she was now the mistress. The children were gone for the day, but there was still work for her to do. It had been her second month of teaching and she had succeeded in overcoming the nervousness she'd initially felt as she took control of the class in the small brick building that served as the new district school.

It had been easier to secure the position than she'd expected as the labor shortage in this growing city included educated teachers.

She'd picked Adelaide without any particular reason. There had been a ship traveling that way and she'd made a split decision to buy passage, primarily for the reason that it was in the direct opposite direction from London. Samson's death had been unexpected and she'd had to make a decision about what to do, and the choices were to go back to her imprisonment or to set out on her own. The second option was infinitely frightening, but on reflection, it was a preferred option to returning to her husband.

The thought of her husband made her frown; she liked it better when she didn't think of him, and Samson had been very good at pushing him from her thoughts. She'd spent too many years worrying about her husband and she was finished. She had been finished the minute she'd decided to leave his house in Devon.

She thought back on the man who had taken her away, her lovely Samson. He'd been attentive and sweet, and above all else, he'd actually liked her. There had been a few others who'd expressed interest in her before Samson, but she'd never encouraged them in the slightest and even looked down on them for expressing interest in a married woman. Even though she had disliked it on the rare occasion when she was discreetly propositioned, it had always shocked her that someone would show interest in her when her husband had consistently proven that there was nothing of interest or of value in her. But then Samson had come along, looked at her as if she was a woman and made her feel alive. She hadn't encouraged him at first, but his interest had introduced forbidden thoughts to her mind.

Focusing her thoughts on the present, she packed away the book that had served as her guide over the last two months—the book in which was written everything she could remember about her own education at a school for privileged young girls. She'd received a good education; her father had secured the best education available to girls not strictly of the right background—that unforgivable sin that had plagued her throughout most of her life, including her marriage.

Turning the heavy lock on the door to her classroom, she headed out onto the dusty street and toward the women's boarding house where she'd established herself since she'd first arrived. Adelaide wasn't a large city, but it was growing—fed by the gold that had been extracted from the state over the last couple of decades. The city was an array of new buildings to show off the prosperity of the inhabitants. Adele couldn't help but to feel the underlying belief in new possibilities and the optimism the people of this town lent to everything they did. They knew they were building a city for the future and were planning on making it a good city, which provided opportunities—even for lone women arriving with nothing but themselves and a change of clothes.

She'd spent most of the journey recovering from the illness that had inflicted her and claimed the man she had

29

been living with for the last six months. She'd fallen sick first and he'd cared for her, ignoring his own worsening condition. And while she started to recover, he'd only grown worse. She'd tried her best to care for him, but the thoughts of her own weakness contributing to his deterioration plagued her. The doctor who'd come to see them had informed her that recovery from the condition was more an issue of personal constitution than anything that could be done for the sufferer, but she still wondered if there was something more she could have done.

His death had been some of the darkest days she'd ever known. She'd forced her weak but recovering body to follow him to the site where he was cremated, hating every single moment of it, but she didn't want to desert him.

Walking home through the streets of Adelaide, the dark and sorrowful memories followed her all the way to the white painted gate of the boarding house. She'd never lived so modestly, but it wasn't the lack of luxuries that bothered her, more the worry about having done the right thing. She had devised a fairly grave deception by letting it be known that she had succumbed to the cholera just like Samson had. She'd had to involve the hotel manager in the deception, but he'd assured her that it wouldn't be a difficult ruse under the circumstances.

She hadn't really known what she was doing. The hotel manager had been kind in trying to console her and she'd confided her fears in returning to her husband— knowing it was the one thing she couldn't do. In response to her distress, he had helped her devise a plan that would release her—release everyone from the obligations they had all been living with.

*

"Come on, Tabitha," a handsome man said, yelling up at the window to Adele's neighbor's room. "You can't be angry with me. It didn't mean a thing."

Adele walked past the man who received no response to his plea. As she reached the porch and stepped inside the door, she looked back briefly at the clearly distressed man, gripping his hat in his hands.

"Is he still out there?" Tabitha asked as they met on the internal staircase.

"Yes."

"What does he take me for? He goes off with another girl and then expects me to take him back when she rejects him. The nerve of the man." Tabitha twirled her dark hair around her finger. "I swear they think they can talk themselves out of anything they do. He charged in here like the cavalry until Matron chased him out with a broom." Tabitha stepped aside on the narrow staircase and let Adele pass. "Really, there are more men here than there are fish in the sea, and he expects me to forgive him."

"Doesn't sound like someone you want to associate with anyway," Adele said.

"He was wonderful at first, and maybe, looking back on it, that should have told me something," Tabitha said as she followed Adele up the stairs.

"I suppose if they are too charming, they've had too much practice."

"Never mind. Move onto the next, I say. We are going to the theater tomorrow night. I think you should come," Tabitha stated. "All the girls are going."

"I don't know," Adele said with uncertainty. She hadn't participated in the social activities devised by the girls of the boarding house.

"You can't sit in your room forever. Would your husband want you to waste your life sitting in your room mourning for him?"

Adele had told people she was a widow when she'd arrived and the persona seemed to have stuck. She didn't feel proud of the deception, but she couldn't very well say that she'd falsified reports of her own death to escape her husband. She knew full well that none of the things she'd done were honorable and she wasn't proud of it, but she needed to be free.

Luckily, no-one asked too many questions about what people did before they reached Australia. Everyone here was from somewhere else and everyone had hopes and dreams that drove them across half of the world to restart their lives in a new country. Tabitha was from Cork and she had come over through a scheme offering free passage for nurses.

"I'm not taking no for an answer—you're coming with us," Tabitha said, pushing open her own door.

"I'll think about it," Adele said, but Tabitha had already closed her door.

Putting her bag down on the table, Adele sank down in the single chair her small room would accommodate. Even with its modest size, the white paper and yellow curtains made it look bright and cheery. The boarding house she'd chosen was a little more expensive than others, but the decor and the insistence on professional women boarders made it a nice place to live. She had walked past a few that seemed to accommodate more rowdy boarders, passing without a second glance.

She'd known this was the one, even as she walked up the path. It was managed by a Mrs. Muiller, who everyone called Matron. She ran a strict curfew and equally strict rules about men even coming up on the porch.

Adele sighed as she still heard the man outside calling for Tabitha to come deal with him, followed by Matron's stern chiding. The man's yelps indicating that he was being taken to by Matron's broom again.

She tried to imagine who would come off best in a confrontation between Matron and her husband. His disapproving looks could wilt anyone, but he would have to compete with Matron's complete lack of sympathy for any male.

*

Adele sat in Isobel's splendid parlor with Isobel and her teenage son, Andrew. The gentle pops of the fire soothing after the large supper they'd had.

"Why don't you stay here tonight? There is no point in you trudging through the sleet all the way home when you will be just as comfortable here," Isobel said.

"I do have the carriage; I would hardly be trudging."

"I am afraid you will have to, because I already dismissed the driver and the footman. It is Christmas after all. I didn't mean to take your stay for granted, but I just didn't have the heart to make them stay."

Adele laughed. "No, you are right; I should have thought of it myself." In truth, staying the night here was a relief in a way as there was little chance that she would run into Lysander, or even that it would surpass anything beyond a greeting if she did, but still, it released the nervous tension she felt whenever she was near or even had the potential of seeing her husband.

"Now shall we sing?" Isobel suggested.

"Really mother, must we?" Andrew said with annoyance.

"Alas, I am going to believe you are impatient at receiving your presents like you used to be, Andrew." The young man groaned with discomfiture of which part, Adele was sure, was put on. "The sad truth is that you will always be my baby and I refuse to acknowledge that you have grown into a man, particularly now at

Christmas when you are required to participate in any delusion I wish to present to myself. There will come a day, you know, when you will miss a mother fussing over you."

"Mother," Andrew hissed with embarrassment.

"Yes well, it is bad enough that you cannot sing like an angel as you used to. Do you remember that Adele, when Andrew would sing at Christmas and his voice was sweet and high like a crisp Christmas bell?" Adele knew that Isobel liked to tease Andrew regarding his embarrassment of his childhood preferences. "These will be your sweetest of memories," she continued.

"It is true," Adele admitted. "The memories of your family Christmas evenings are some of the sweetest you will carry with you, particularly after you lose them." The loss of her parents still sat heavily in her chest and it was the reason why Isobel had insisted that Adele spend the Christmas season in town this year.

"But I will await the day when you are happy to sing for us again, Andrew. Until then, we will overlook the singing, just this once. Perhaps your singing voice will return when there is a girl here who you wish to impress, hmm?"

"Mother," Andrew groaned yet again.

"Very well, we will open the presents."

Andrew wasn't quite old enough that the idea of presents didn't overrule his perpetual dismay with the world and everyone in it. Andrew took charge at this point and sorted out the presents to their rightful intendant, while the women looked on. It was clear to see the adoration on Isobel's face—a state she could only indulge in when he wasn't looking.

Andrew received Adele's stationery set for his studies and a fishing set, along with a fine pair of riding boots. Isobel preferred to save her presents for later, while Adele received three presents. The first an oriental shawl from Andrew and then a pair of kidskin gloves from Isobel. The third box, she knew what it contained by the noise it made. It was the cherry brandy chocolates from Fortnum and Mason that her husband gave to her every year. She unwrapped the present, but didn't open the box. She'd never liked them, but she received them each year without fail. The shiny chocolates looked like dark little jewels, but each year she hoped he would get her something different. She knew they were expensive, but it didn't change the fact that she didn't like them and her husband either didn't know or didn't care. She always preferred to think that he just wasn't aware of her dislike for them, but then she wasn't entirely certain that it was him who'd bought them, or his secretary Wilson.

Chapter 4

"WHERE IS MY WIFE'S BODY?" Lysander asked with increasing annoyance as he sat in the Colonial Office's Calcutta headquarters. There was a fan over his head moving air around the space, operated by a man standing on the other side of the room. It did nothing to dissipate the pressing heat. His vexation and the blasted heat of the place were making him feel faint. He never fainted, but this unrelenting humidity was taxing in ways his body couldn't handle. He hated feeling weak and this place made him feel less than at his best.

"I have spoken to the medical staff who cared for the couple—" Mr. Parsons caught himself and winced, "sorry, your wife and her ... companion." Lysander closed his eyes with the embarrassment and sheer unbelievability of this whole situation, which had quickly turned into a farce. "A Doctor Smith had seen them both and they were both quite ill."

"And then?" Lysander pressed.

"We received word from the hotel that the pair had passed away." Mr. Parsons produced a note and placed it in front of him. Lysander leaned forward, reading the note. It stated simply that two of the hotel's guests had died and it stated their names.

"In the case of cholera," Mr. Parsons went on, "it is imperative that the infectiousness of the bodies is handled at the earliest opportunity to minimize the spread of contagion. Normally bodies are brought back to the coroner, but in the case of highly infectious diseases, it is important to deal with the bodies immediately. The coroner does sometimes depend on the input of dependable witnesses. I am sorry to have to discuss such delicate and uncomfortable topics."

"I don't care about discomfort, Mr. Parsons. What makes me uncomfortable is not knowing where my wife's body went. You are telling me that the hotel manager was the last, and the only person to see my wife's body."

"We can only assume that she was taken to another place to be cremated. We do not have a crematorium of our own as local practices have served sufficient for these rare moments ..." Mr. Parsons trailed off. "I will make some inquiries along the river to see if we can locate where her body was ... where her pyre was."

"And what of the woman?"

"What woman?"

"The one who attended the cremation of Mr. Ellingwood."

"Perhaps one of the hotel staff?"

"Come now, Mr. Parsons, there are no white women serving at the hotel."

"Another guest perhaps?"

"Following the cholera victims through the city? I dare say not."

"Then what are you saying, my Lord?"

Lysander didn't answer, but had a suspicion boring through his mind. It had been his first thought when he'd first heard that there was a woman watching the cremation, and there was no female body. But on further thinking, he had dismissed it. His wife was a stickler for etiquette and for following every archaic rule of propriety; he couldn't see her knowingly doing something like this. Then again, he had never expected her to run off with a lover either.

Maybe it had been his wife watching her lover's pyre. Maybe she had mistakenly been declared dead and was innocently unaware of the mistake. But then, where was she?

Perhaps she was on her way to England. The thought made him angry—he had come all this way for a simple clerical error. This only fed into the underlying anger that she had done this—embarrassed him in the way she had. He was fairly sure he would never forgive this further imposition.

Bidding goodbye to Mr. Parsons, he returned to the hotel and the peaceful tranquillity it presented in the middle of the sheer chaos that was Calcutta. He needed a bath; he could smell the smoke of the riverside sticking to his clothes like the clothes stuck to his body, wet with sweat.

*

Lysander requested the attention of the hotel manager when he arrived back, after ordering a gin and tonic in the bar.

"I understand you saw my wife's body after her death," Lysander said as the man appeared. The man didn't respond immediately.

"Yes," he said after a moment of silence. "And I wish to relay my deepest condolences."

Lysander nodded, but there was something in the man's demeanor—judgment.

"And you are sure you saw her?"

"I didn't look very closely, but I am sure it was your wife's body. Again, I am very sorry for your loss. If that is all, I am afraid I must go attend to some repairs." He smiled discreetly and withdrew. Lysander decided that he didn't entirely trust this man—there was something in the way the man regarded him, but then maybe that wasn't out of line considering his wife had been living here with another man. Perhaps a bit of judgment was to be expected under the circumstances—it would be were the roles reversed.

Returning to his room, Lysander went through his late wife's possessions. There was nothing out of the ordinary. Surely if she'd left, she wouldn't leave all these things behind. Clothes, toiletries and even jewelry. He noted that the wedding band wasn't there, but then he wasn't sure she would have brought it with her when leaving to live with another man. It must be back at the Hall, he assumed. Then he noted that there wasn't a hair brush. There was a comb amongst Mr. Ellingwood's effects, but no hair brush amongst his wife's. While he didn't know his wife well, he knew women well enough to know they cared for their hair. There was the possibility that his wife would have used Mr. Ellingwood's comb, but not for the period of months they were together.

It could, of course, have been stolen, but then the jewelry was still present. The realization only confirmed suspicions he couldn't quite have formulated before. There was no body of his wife, a woman had been watching Mr. Ellingwood's cremation and now the most crucial item of women's personal care was missing. It could possibly be that his wife was alive and that she had conducted a deception; although this could all be his imagination conjuring a fantastical turn of events.

He didn't know what to do, feeling boxed in at every turn. His wife was either alive and deceiving him, or she was dead and lost. He didn't honestly know what was required of him, but something was—he had to deal with this. Either way, he had to find her before he was free of this whole affair.

*

The hotel manager was indisposed when he next tried to seek him out, making Lysander narrow his eyes when the message was conveyed to him. He suspected he would get no more assistance from the man and if he did, he wasn't sure he could trust it. If his wife was alive, this man had possibly attested to her death knowing it was a deception.

He further mulled over the character of the woman who would do such a thing, the character of the woman who was his wife, in name if nothing more. He wasn't entirely sure which outcome he wanted, but it would probably be easier if she was deceased. A deception of this magnitude could not be born; it signified a flaw in character beyond anything tolerable.

Returning to the train station, he made inquiries regarding lone women buying tickets, but there were none fitting the description of his wife. The only other place was the port. Gritting his teeth through the rickshaw ride, he moved past the cacophony of life existing on the streets of this city. He was getting a bit more accustomed to the complete assault on his senses each time he left the lush, green surroundings of the hotel, and familiarity of what was outside was alleviating some of the distress.

Occasionally he would pass others—British men and women in their light dresses and suits—heading off in rickshaws to whatever business they had. He tipped his hat to each in an odd gesture of familiarity with people he had essentially not met before, but the foreignness of the place encouraged an odd sense of familiarity even with perfect strangers—perhaps because they lived with the same exotic experiences here. The same had been true with the other guests at the hotel. There was a feeling of camaraderie brought on by the fact that they were British in a foreign place. A few of the hotel guests were residents living there on a permanent or a semi-permanent basis, like Adele and Mr. Ellingwood had—working here and raising their families. It was Britain, but it was different—the rules were different and the lines of demarcation within English society appeared to be much more blurry here.

The port was as busy and unpleasant as expected. There were people, goods and carts moving in every available space. It took him a while, but he found a spectacled young Indian man in the port building to help him make inquiries amongst the passenger agents. The man encouraged him to sit in a chair while a glass of tea was presented to him.

Sitting back, Lysander watched the frantic activity across the dock area while he waited for the man to return. It took close to an hour, but the young man returned to confirm that there had indeed been a young woman by the name of A. Ellis, traveling alone during the time period in question—to Adelaide.

Lysander frowned. *Adelaide?* he repeated to himself. He couldn't really see Adele traveling to Adelaide. It couldn't possibly be further away from London. She had no ties with Adelaide—or even with Australia. It didn't make sense; she would cut off any support she had, travel to the ends of the earth and for what? The only thing he knew about Adelaide was that there was gold there; although he could hardly see her as a gold prospector. The whole notion of Adele traveling to Adelaide was ludicrous.

He queried if there were any other young women traveling alone, but there were none, except a diplomatic wife traveling to Peking. He dismissed the idea of the diplomatic wife, but the other was harder to dismiss. Adelaide would be a place where someone would go to shed their identity. He wasn't ready to believe it was Adele, but he had to concede that there was something in his gut that identified with this person.

Seeking out another rickshaw, he made his way back to the hotel to change and refresh before his supper with the Viceroy.

*

Lysander arrived at Government House shortly after dusk—a massive building not much different from many stately homes back in England. His carriage drew up in front of a large sandstone staircase, where staff were waiting to

41

assist. An aide showed him the way to the Brown Dining Room, where the evening's event was being held. The halls held portraits or paintings of a myriad of royals and also previous Viceroys.

It had been a long day and he was both tired and hungry. If it had been up to him, he would have preferred staying close to his room, but when such distinguished persons extended invitations, it was plain rude to decline, particularly on short notice for no discernible reason.

"Warburton, good to see you," Viceroy Mayo said as he was shown into the brightly lit dining room holding a collection of people. There were women in elegant and light silk dresses and men in light suits made for the climate. He considered whether he should have some made for himself, but his short stay didn't justify a new wardrobe and he didn't want to stay to wait for it to be ready. "Ghastly business about your wife."

"Yes," Lysander agreed as he was delivered a drink on a silver tray.

"Has Parsons been able to locate her?"

"Not that I have heard."

"Then I hear the woman had a habit of getting lost," the Viceroy said. Lysander knew the statement indicating that the Viceroy was aware of her presence in Calcutta and the circumstances in which she was living.

"So it seems," Lysander returned non-committally. He'd grown used to veiled comments about his wife over the last ten months. It was embarrassing, but there was nothing he could do to counter the accusation—it was true after all.

"I am sure Parsons will find her, or rather where she was joined with the river as the locals say. He is having the Imperial Police Service assist with scouring the city. I have no doubt they will find some further information shortly."

Lysander had met Lord Mayo on a number of occasions previously. He'd made an appearance in London on a frequent basis as it had always been a part of his role as the Secretary for Ireland. He was an excellent administrator and the position of Viceroy was well-deserved and well-allocated. "Come eat. You can tell us of any gossip from London."

It was a pleasant supper and he relayed what he knew for the benefit of the ladies present. He usually didn't pay close attention to the stories that amused women, but he told them what he could. When they asked him about the latest fashion, he was frankly lost.

"Now for some whiskey while the women refresh themselves," Lord Mayo said. The men moved over to a set of chairs along a stretch of the balcony that surrounded the large building. The air was pleasant this time of night—not stifling, but a warm breeze that was welcome after the harsh sun of the day.

The men talked about some reforms aimed to educate the general local population while they sipped Irish whiskey that Lord Mayo had shipped over throughout the year. "One must have some home comforts or one goes mad," he explained as he urged the servers to refill their glasses. "It is good to see you, Warburton. What do you think of our fair city?"

"I am getting used to its activity."

Lord Mayo laughed. "One never gets used to it, but one does miss it upon return to gentler environments, I hear." Lysander wasn't sure he was prepared to believe that. "I couldn't convince you to stay? We need good men. In particular, I need a Lieutenant Governor for Andaman and Nicobar. It's a savage place that needs to be brought under control."

"A task I fear would be beyond me," Lysander said with jovial certainty. He wasn't a man who craved such adventure and he had no desire to spend years in some savage foreign land, particularly a prison colony.

"Shame," the Viceroy said with disappointment. "I was hoping for someone of a less military background for the position. Those military men do tend to approach tasks with a lack of circumspection at times. No offense, Hargeston." A man who was apparently of military persuasion raised his glass in acceptance.

"I met your wife," one of the other men said. "Lovely woman and a wonderful wit. Such a shame she succumbed."

"Yes," Lysander said without elaborating. The statement surprised him as he hadn't realized that Adele and her lover were socializing. It wasn't something that would have been possible in London, but again, the rules were different here—more relaxed and flexible. He knew that his wife and Mr. Ellingwood were not the only couple in unfortunate circumstances who sought a life in India.

He wondered how long they would have stayed here; if they planned on making this their home. He also didn't recognize the woman who they had described meeting either—she sounded like a perfect stranger. Adele wasn't a lovely woman, or even a memorable woman as far as he saw, but the people who met her here saw her differently. Perhaps it was Samson Ellingwood who'd brought this change in her, he thought as he downed the last of his whiskey.

Chapter 5

"COME ON, GIRLS, IT'S TIME TO GO," Tabitha said impatiently down in the foyer, while Adele followed Rosie down the stairs.

"We're coming," Rosie yelled back with annoyance. "Are you afraid you're going to miss something?"

"The start, and I don't want the worst seats in the house." Tabitha shooed them all out of the door and onto the darkening street outside. The setting sun was not quieting the streets where the daily life of moving goods was replaced by people seeking amusement outside their homes.

They normally went for leisurely walks at this time of evening, but tonight they were going to see a play called the Colleen Bawn. Adele had been uncertain about going along, but Tabitha had been true to her word and would not take no for an answer. Adele would normally join them if they were going for a walk, but typically declined if they had more extensive plans.

She was actually nervous, feeling as if she was doing something she shouldn't. Women like her didn't go to the theater, but she wasn't women like her anymore; she was something else and for the type of person she was here, it was perfectly acceptable for her to go to the theater for the evening with a group of female companions.

The theater was actually more wholesome here than it was in London, where it was the focal point of less admirable activities. It was somewhere Lysander took his mistress—a place where it was acceptable to be seen by others with women who weren't strictly acceptable in the drawing-rooms of society.

The newly installed gas lights lit their way as the darkness took over, casting semicircles of light on the dusty road heading into the center of town. It was a pleasant city in the evenings, a bit chilly, but it didn't have the rawness that London had most of the year. Adele had missed London when she'd lived in Devon and she rarely got to visit. While she had grown up in London, she had seldom had the opportunity to explore—being shifted between tutors and schools, her life was regimented, and amusement was typically not part of her day.

She looked over at her companions who were dressed in their best dresses for the evening. The Sunday church dresses were supposed to be their best, but that wasn't true—these were their best dresses, the dresses they were seen in on nights out. Rosie looked beautiful with her pale complexion and blonde hair. Tabitha was very pretty as well, but in a more unconventional way. In all, they made for an attractive group and they caught the eyes of the men they passed.

Adele was still not used to the way men regarded women here—more direct and confronting as a consequence of the sheer number of males in the city compared to females. It was a city of youth and energy, and women had their pick of men—not that Adele was interested in picking a man. She wasn't interested in another relationship and the loss of Samson was still fresh in her mind.

She had adored Samson and he had been a perfect gentleman to her in all things. He'd said he would have married her of it was possible, but they both suspected that her husband wasn't going to release her—and Lysander was too young to widow her anytime soon. Samson had harmed his career by being with her and she had worried endlessly over that fact, but he insisted that he would do it again if given the chance.

Samson had accepted the harm to his career and for that, Adele would be forever grateful to him. She hoped she had loved him enough for his faith and belief in her. She wasn't entirely convinced she deserved it, but he had given freely. He'd shown her intimacy and the delights of the bedroom, which she had learnt to crave. His love and support had brought out a different side to her and she enjoyed just being with him, and it didn't matter what they did, she was just happy. Being with him was easy; he was never gloomy or lamenting, always contented with what was available to them at the time. He was so very different from Lysander. Lysander didn't strive for change, but he was never contented—at least not in her presence; if he was with his mistress, she wasn't sure. She wasn't privy to his life in any way; she only heard things from others.

The only thing Adele regretted from the time she spent with Samson was that he hadn't given her a child. Her life would be complete her if she had a child to care for. It had been something she'd hoped for since the very start of her marriage, but her husband hadn't wanted to spend the time with her needed to ensure that happened.

*

The theater was brightly lit when they arrived. There were people waiting outside and they arrived just in time for the doors to open.

"They are going to close the theater soon," Tabitha said.

"Why?" Rosie said with concern.

"They're building a new one—a spectacular one."

"But we will be without a theater."

"For a while."

"Why can't they just leave well enough alone?"

"Because this just isn't grand enough, apparently."

47

Adele looked around the decor and she did see the point. Even with her limited experience, she could tell that compared to London's theaters, this was very simple. There was only painting on the walls and ceilings, and they weren't expertly done. There wasn't a gold leaf in sight. In fact, it was a humble theater and the people of Adelaide must have decided that it didn't do them justice.

"We'll just have to find other ways of amusing ourselves." Tabitha's eyes narrowed as she watched a man across the hall. It was the same man who had been calling for her on their lawn the other evening. He was there with a blond woman with horsy teeth. "That took all of two minutes," Tabitha said with distaste. "Good riddance."

The theater itself was slightly dusty and the leather-covered chairs looked well-worn. They took seats in the center of the theater while Rosie was distracted by two men whom she obviously knew.

"She is such a flirt," Tabitha stated. "You should take a few lessons from her. You're not planning on being the mourning widow forever, are you? Some man will come along and sweep you off your feet."

"I think I will just stick to being a simple school teacher for now." Adele wasn't sure she could handle an entanglement with another man; she'd relinquished her whole life and she was unable to bear the emotional turmoil of another relationship right now. While her time with Samson had been lovely and fulfilling, getting to that point had been a difficult process.

The heavy velvet curtains drew back and the play started. Adele didn't know much of the play other than it had first shown in New York before traveling across the world. It started and the characters were introduced, starting with a nobleman who had a secret wife living across a lake—one he loved but was ashamed of. Adele frowned as

48

the plot of the play developed. He admonished the girl for her peasant ways when he was really upset that he couldn't marry a lovely and also wealthy noblewoman whose attention was being vied for by a number of characters.

Adele couldn't stop the play from resonating with her own situation. There was a distinct difference in that the character in the play did or had loved this woman he had married in secret. This was a huge point of difference with her own life, because her husband had never loved her. She hadn't immediately realized Lysander's dislike and contempt for her. He'd been beautiful and perfect when he had first been introduced to her.

*

Adele looked up at the facade of the house in Mayfair as they arrived right on time. Her father had been very nervous for this dinner and he'd even come and advised her on the dress she was to wear.

"This is a very important dinner," he'd said to her gravely. "We are meeting the Warburtons—a very important and distinguished family. Their importance goes back for generations and having association with them shows a distinct improvement in the position of our family name."

They'd arrived in her father's best carriage, which was newly imported from France with dark burgundy lacquer reflecting every point of light. Father was very proud of this carriage and would use it anytime he wished to impress someone. Adele suspected that her father would have dearly liked to have a family crest to paint on its side, but it was instead decorated with some elegant swirls in a special metallic paint brought over from Russia.

They were dressed in the latest Parisian fashion and Adele knew her dress was gorgeous. As it turned out, they were better dressed than the family they were there to meet, having been shown into a parlor where they were introduced to the family—a man, his sister and a son. The house was older and less sumptuous than their

49

own, but these people were better than them, irrespective of how richly decorated their possessions were. It was an inescapable fact that this family was of the right background and they were of the wrong, and all the money in the world wouldn't change that.

Adele showed every politeness as had been ingrained in her from a young age. Her school had ensured that she knew every point of etiquette for handling herself in just such situation as this. She knew she would embarrass her father if she did anything wrong and she had to combat her nerves to calm her mind, but she couldn't dismiss the fact that she was quietly terrified.

Their son was young and handsome, maybe even the most handsome man Adele had ever met. He had brown hair perfectly cut, blue eyes and strong features. He cut an attractive figure as he looked relaxed if not a little bored sitting on one of the settees. His forefinger played with the rim of his glass as they chatted lightly, prior to being called by the dinner bell. Adele noted how different his hand was to hers—bigger and stronger, and masculine. She had never noticed a man's hands before, but she noticed his.

In his presence, she felt self-conscious, but she was spared from notice, although she was placed opposite him when the dinner bell was finally rung. His clear eyes scanned the table and Adele looked down to her lap every time his gaze went anywhere near her. Her breath hitch whenever he would look at her and she was sure her face blushed to show it.

The men discussed politics and business throughout the dinner. Lysander had a clear, deep voice and an obvious distaste for some of the political maneuvering that had been consuming everyone's attention of late.

She joined her mother and Lord Warburton's sister, Isobel, when it was time for the women to retreat to the parlor. The woman chatted about some landscaping changes that were proposed for Hyde Park. Isobel was kind enough, but even the light conversation couldn't make up for the fact that they were virtual strangers.

When it was time to say farewell, Adele's hand shook slightly as Lysander obligingly took her hand and kissed the knuckles of her fingers. His lips only made the barest of touch, but Adele didn't care; it made her heart race all the same.

"That man will be your husband," her father said when the carriage had taken off down the street. Adele blinked to take in the astounding information; it didn't seem real. When she imagined her husband, she hadn't even contemplated someone as handsome and intelligent as Lysander Warburton. Collecting herself, she felt her breath and heartbeat quicken as she absorbed the news. She had never in her wildest dreams hoped for such a match and she didn't even dare think about how well her future looked.

*

Adele watched the scene unfold when the nobleman's friend tried to have the peasant girl murdered to free his friend to marry the well-placed and beautiful noblewoman. Adele felt her heart constrict. She wanted to leave, not just the play, but all the feelings it brought out of her, but she was stuck. There were people on both sides of her and she would disrupt the whole room if she got up and insisted people let her get out of the row.

Instead, she closed her eyes and tried to think of Samson and all the good things he had brought to her life. Thinking of her husband hurt and she hadn't come all this way for that hurt to follow her. She should have tried harder to decline the evening and this was her punishment for not standing her ground, staying well and safe in her little room. She liked her small life here; it was simple and it was easy.

The play ended with the nobleman lamenting how his wife had been treated and they left happily together. Love prevailed and conquered. Real life wasn't like that, she knew. Love didn't always win; sometimes it lost.

Chapter 6

ADELAIDE'S PORT WASN'T THE same degree of chaos that India had been and he silently thanked the fates for it. He felt that even the long voyage here hadn't been enough to recover from the assault on the senses that was India. The port was busy, but orderly and there were carriages for hire waiting patiently to transport new arrivals to the city. After engaging one, Lysander watched the countryside pass. It was again so very different from what he knew, and he couldn't quite believe that he was on the opposite side of the globe. The plants were different; the birds were different and the light was also different. It seemed his wife had led him on a merry chase around the world—if she indeed was his wife.

The town was also different from what he'd expected—not that he had many expectations, but it was all new, built in the latest architectural style—a completely modern town, with meticulously planned and maintained streets, and large parklands between neighborhoods. He didn't see telephone lines, which were being rolled out across London, so they were behind London in that respect.

His countenance darkened when he considered the reason he was there—to chase down a woman who may or may not be his wife. In his gut, he knew it was. He wasn't sure why; he'd never observed any deviousness in her, but looking back, her constant cool reserve was bound to hide something. Perhaps that was just the nature of her class, he thought maliciously. It was an unfair assumption, but he felt he needed something to funnel his anger toward.

Taking rooms in a nice hotel in the center of the city, he would convalesce after his long journey. The hotel had all the services he would require—even good quality Ceylon tea that he was partial to. It served a mix of clientele, but that was typical of hotels in far-flung places, he'd noted.

After he was sufficiently recovered, he sent out a note to the Town Hall to enquire about a new female entrant in the community by the name of A. Ellis. He had to admire the efficiency when a note returned only a few hours later saying that Mrs. Adele Ellis was now a teacher at the school in Young Ward's Gilles Street.

Scrunching up the note, Lysander threw it in the fire. Surely that couldn't be his wife? There had to be some mistake, an innocent mistake that he would laugh at later. His wife was dead and her body lost due to some mishap in the chaos of India—that made sense. Him chasing after some ghost across the world didn't. He should turn back, go home and forget all about this. But he couldn't; he was here and he had to see this through. It was his duty.

The carriage delivered him to a small wooden building that was the school house, with two windows, one on each side of the door. It certainly was different from his education at Eton, where old, hallowed walls steeped in tradition, told of their place and responsibility. This was a small little house—a true education here seemed impossible.

The door was painted light blue and it creaked as he opened it. A few blemishes scarred the door that was otherwise new. Children, he realized—they were rough on everything. Not a topic he usually considered—likely because the idea of acquiring them by his wife had been so unappealing.

The door opened to a large room where light shone in on a woman who was tidying a desk along the far wall. She wore a brown gingham dress with a tightly corseted bodice and a large skirt. With clear relief, he knew instantly that he'd made a mistake—until the woman looked up and he saw the face of his wife. The picture didn't make sense for a second—the face, the place and the dress didn't match.

Her eyes widened and he saw fear in them. Blood rushed to his head, making him feel light-headed. A rush of dark emotion overwhelmed his ability to speak, but he moved forward to her and took her by the neck when he reached her.

"You liar," he managed to spit out. Her eyes were still large and disbelieving. "Do you have any idea of the embarrassment you've caused me? You've made me the laughing stock of London. You deceptive whore." He was babbling, not really knowing what was coming out of his mouth, but all the suppressed anger and embarrassment flooded out of him. Being cuckolded by an unworthy man, exposed to the ridicule of everyone he knew, then being deceived to travel across the world in a vain effort to show her memory some respect. And this is how he was treated.

"You dress up in the guise of a respectable school teacher when we both know that is far from the truth. Do you think any of the parents of these children would like an adulteress and deceiver teaching their children? This dress looks ridiculous on you. You are ridiculous."

Her mouth parted slightly as if she wanted to say something, her lips were pink and plump. A mouth she'd given to other men, and who knew how many he didn't know about. Her thin neck was warm under his hand. He was affecting her ability to draw breath and he didn't care at that particular moment. An impulse to squeeze flashed through him and it was tempting. Her large eyes were pleading with him.

And then there was that matter of her not being dead, which meant she was again his wife and his problem to deal with. A problem from the start to the very end. Why had he been afflicted with this burden? An unsuitable and untrue wife. He could see her with her man in that room in Calcutta, giving herself to him with abandon. He felt pure rage. The whore.

Before he knew what he was doing, he had her skirt bunched up around her stomach, wrestling with her as he exposed her legs. "If you insist on behaving like a whore, perhaps I should treat you like one. Her hands gripped his wrists, fighting him. Something in the back of his mind told him it wasn't so, but he was too angry to listen—his emotions at such extreme levels he couldn't think or reason. The feeling was unbearable, cutting off air to his lungs and blood to his mind.

A sharp slap brought him to his senses, informing him that in his rage, he had just about forced himself on his wife in a most brutal fashion. Violence in its purest form. Collapsing down on the desk, his put his hands out on either side of her as she still tried to fight him off, clearly terrified. He felt faint, unsure what had just happened or how he had gotten there—too tired to think of anything.

Stepping back, he surveyed her as she lay on the desk trying to push her skirt down to cover her modesty. To cover what he had almost just done. She wasn't looking at him, her cheeks rosy with embarrassment or distress, or whatever it was she was feeling. Frowning deeply, he felt a stab of guilt, but he was too depleted to feel anything properly. Anger still licked at his consciousness, but there simply wasn't room for emotions.

"Outside," he ordered as his breath grew calm enough for a steady voice. He didn't want to think anymore—about what he'd just done, what she'd done or the implications of the future. And there were implications for the future. His devious and faithless wife back in his life. If only he'd turned around this morning and returned to England in ignorant bliss, but now he knew and there was no undoing that. She was his responsibility, no matter how she acted.

She slowly stood, her eyes lowered to the floor. He wasn't sure if her modesty was because of shame for what had just happened, or simply for that she'd been found out. Anger tickled him again, but he couldn't rise to it. He lifted his hand to the door to urge her to walk, which she did, taking tentative steps past him.

*

He had his possessions moved to a different suite, one with two bedrooms. She'd argued that she had a room somewhere, but he didn't trust her not to run off—not entirely sure what she was capable of anymore. He didn't want her in his bed, but he didn't trust her being out of sight either. With her in the room across from him, he would hear if she left her bedroom. He wasn't sure that was true, but he certainly wasn't going to share a room with her.

"We're leaving in the morning," he stated when they were showed into their suite for the evening. "We're sailing for Europe." He'd sent one of the hotel's boys to seek information on passage, promising to pay handsomely for the service as he wasn't feeling up to dealing with the matter himself just at that moment. He needed to sleep, feeling the need tug at him as he watched the creature who was his wife stand by the window, surveying the scene outside.

"Can I get my things?" she asked quietly.

"No." It was ungenerous, but he didn't want to deal with it. He had no idea what she held precious, probably gifts from her lover. He wasn't going to traipse across town for that. Then he softened slightly. "If there is enough time in the morning, you can send a man to collect them."

They existed in silence for a while until supper was brought to their room and served at the table. They ate in silence and Lysander read the evening paper the hotel had supplied.

Lying in bed that night, he was unable to sleep. He had his wife back. It wasn't a welcome development, but he couldn't shirk his responsibility. Closing his eyes in a vain attempt to sleep, he considered what he would do with her when he returned. No solutions came to mind. It was all just one big jumble of unpleasantness. There was always the gossip resulting from her return to look forward to. If her latest caper became known, she—and he, by association— would become notorious. Faking one's own death was dramatics on an unprecedented scale. But people knew of her demise and her appearance will cause quite a stir. The only thing he could do was to stand by the idea that it was a clerical error. He despised lies, but the alternative was unbearable.

Chapter 7

ADELE STEPPED OUT OF THE carriage at the Port of Melbourne. She'd watched the landscape pass by, wishing she had a chance to explore the city they'd arrived in just the previous day. Lysander showed no interest in the city and they hadn't left the hotel until it was time to leave.

He'd been uniformly distant, but not unpleasant to her. She wondered if he ignored her presence most of the time. He read each edition of the paper made available and intermittently retreated to the smoking room, being sternly polite, but he didn't speak to her beyond what she wanted to eat and enquiring if she was comfortable. Later, he even went out and bought some gloves for her when she mentioned that she'd lost her pair.

It was still a relief when he left her alone—not that he purposefully made her uncomfortable—the whole situation was uncomfortable enough without either of them having to try. The worst was that she didn't know what his intentions were. He'd mentioned nothing of divorce, but then he'd mentioned nothing of the future either. His only concern at the moment, it seemed, was to get them back to England. As for what would happen then, she was none the wiser. Surely, he couldn't intend to place her at the Devon house again, to continue as before. They couldn't continue as they had, too much had happened since then, surely.

Adele twisted the handkerchief she held as she looked out on the large ship that was to carry them back to Europe—an auxiliary steamer, which included both sailing masts and two large steam turrets. It was a very sleek ship, unlike any she'd seen before—a large vessel, with black smoke billowing from the chimneys as it was preparing to sail. Lysander urged her toward the gangway which conveyed them to an opening in the front of the ship. Adele could see goods and provisions being loaded onto the ship further down its length. There was also a second entrance further down the ship, utilized by persons of lesser means.

The interior was sumptuous and everything looked new. Every surface was dressed in glass, brass or lacquered mahogany, with rich oriental carpets covering all floors. A smartly uniformed man greeted them and showed them toward their cabins. Their trunks had been sent ahead and were apparently waiting for their arrival.

"Lord and Lady Warburton. I am Mr. Manfred and I wish you welcome to the RMS Oceanic. We are very pleased to have you traveling with us on our grandest ship— the best sailing the oceans. Built for luxury travel, it has a first-class section with splendid walkways and a salon for your entertainment. Your cabins are just here and this is Hans," he said when they came to a man dressed in a dark uniform, "who will take care of any needs you should have while in your cabin. You just have to ring the bell and he will attend you."

To Adele's relief, Lysander had booked them separate cabins and hers was as fine as any hotel room she'd ever seen. His means stretched further than Samson Ellingwood's could.

Pulling off her gloves as the man left her cabin to see to Lysander, she sat down heavily on the bed, feeling her energy drain from her. It had all just become real; she was heading back to the life she had left behind, with the man she had left behind. Or else she was heading back for divorce and the uncertainty and potential poverty that came with it. A divorce would mean the end of her existence in respectable society, but that was a decision she'd already made when she took up with Samson.

She'd thought she'd made her escape, but here she was again—a prisoner in this marriage. Biting the nail of her thumb, she wished she could behave childishly, cry and scream—throw a tantrum to show how displeased she was. But she wasn't a child; she was a married woman, and handling setbacks with grace were part of that responsibility.

She rested for a while, until there was a discreet knock at the door adjoining what she assumed was Lysander's cabin. She knew it was sometimes a feature that was provided to married couples; although she couldn't see her husband utilizing it. It would be a substantial change in their relationship. Although, his reaction when he saw her had been unlike any reaction she'd ever received from him. But she knew it was an act of anger rather than ardor.

"Will you accompany me to the salon for supper?" Lysander asked when she opened the door, his face impassive. "We will be going in half an hour."

Adele felt his eyes on her and they were again neither kind nor hateful—they were just indifferent. Knowing it was a request more than a question, she nodded. Perversely, she wasn't entirely sure which one she preferred, indifference or hatred. They hadn't discussed what had happened—they'd discussed nothing at all. But apparently, he would be associating with her publicly.

She dressed in her yellow gown, which was the only thing she had that was fine enough for dining in a salon, having left all her other worthy dresses back in India as she'd departed for a new life, one she'd assumed wouldn't include fine gowns.

Looking herself over in the mirror, she noted that she looked drawn; although the sun of Australia hid the pallor she would normally have in England. She was still disbelieving at the turn of events, but perhaps this was as it should be and it was her mad escape that had been the unbelievable part.

Lysander was waiting outside when she stepped out of her cabin, closing the door behind her. She'd placed the key in her purse and tentatively took his arm. Touching him felt strange. He'd never seemed quite real to her, but here he was, warm flesh and blood.

They were shown to a large table headed by the Captain—a Captain Harrow, a retired Naval man with a manicured white beard and shrewd eyes. The salon had a large glass dome above their heads, which showed the stars above, and the walls were covered with silk and wood. It was a beautiful room, no expense had been spared in furnishing the ship. The other passengers were a mixed lot, mostly wealthy Australians and some Government officials—people they would be dining with for months.

An elderly woman sat to Adele's left. "Such a lovely couple," the woman said in a voice that had a slight tremor. "Are you on your honeymoon?"

"No, we have been married for some time." The idea that anyone would see them as a lovely couple was strange—they were anything but. It seemed the rift between them wasn't visible to everyone, while Adele would have thought as obvious as a sign floating above their heads.

Turning back to her right, she surveyed the man next to her—her husband, who was being spoken to by a man he didn't approve of, looking arrogant and distant. He was handsome; he always had been and his maturation had not diminished his good looks. It is how she was used to seeing him—arrogant and distant amongst the portraits that covered the walls in the Devon house.

When there, she would stop and look at him whenever she walked past the main hall—the large portrait of him on the left wall. She had stood in front of that portrait countless times. There were another two of him, one as a toddler, which she could never really align in her mind with him, and still another from when he was around sixteen and not yet a man. That portrait in the main hall was more linked to the idea of her husband than the man sitting next to her. She was familiar with all its lines and shadows, the fall of his clothes and the distant look in his eyes. The living man next to her was much more difficult to comprehend.

*

The next morning, Adele sat reading on the shaded side of the ship in a white rattan chair with a cushion to soften the seat. A tea service had been offered and accepted.

Luckily, her absorption into her book seemed to signal to other passengers that her privacy was preferred on this occasion. Sipping the tea, she tried to read, but her jumbled emotions stopped her from focusing. She'd taken the direction that if she ignored her emotions and acted calm, her insides would eventually follow suit.

"There you are," she heard the voice of the man who was her husband. "I wondered where you were."

Adele considered if she was supposed to have told him of her planned activities for the day. "Naturally I am not far away. It is unlikely that I would have jumped the rail to make my escape." They were still traveling along the Australian coastline, but she wasn't quite that daring.

He looked uncomfortable for a moment before sitting down, pulling up the material of his light green traveling suit. They had never traveled together before; she wasn't entirely sure he liked traveling. Having him there was uncomfortable; she didn't know what to say to him. She knew her own crimes as did he. But he had sought her out and she was sure it wasn't to be sociable.

"I wanted to discuss what happened," he started, staring out into the ocean, squinting with the light of the harsh Australian sun. He was clearly not made for this climate. She had struggled with it herself, but had accepted it as her new home. Distracting herself by her thoughts, she knew she wasn't ready for the conversation he was embarking on; it wasn't one she wanted to have. "I am sorry for how I behaved," he said after clearing his throat, looking down at his brown leather shoes. She didn't know where he got his shoes, things a wife should know. She knew none of these things about him. Still, he looked extremely uncomfortable. "I wanted to apologize for how I behaved..." He cleared his throat. "When we were reunited. I have no excuse for it and such behaviour is not normally in my character."

Embarrassment crept up her face as she took in his words and their meaning. She looked away, not wanting to have this discussion or to consider the intentions behind what he'd almost done.

"I can promise such will never happen again."

She wasn't sure she could accept his promise. It was evident that she could push him to the point of grave anger, which she hadn't known was possible. The only emotions she had ever observed in him were annoyance and disapproval.

"I accept your apology," she said stiffly. "We will never speak of it again." Along with his promise, she wasn't sure she did accept his apology either. If his intention were ever to impose on her, he was within his right to do so. But she appreciated his apology, even as it couldn't go far to mend the rift between them, not when the greater grievance had been their marriage and their whole association. The incident for which he was apologizing for was a fleeting moment that, in accordance to his own estimation, was out of character.

Rising, he nodded to her. "I will see you at lunch. You, of course, have the run of the ship for your diversion."

It was an attempt at generosity and she accepted it as such despite its awkwardness. He could, after all, lock her in her cabin and forbid her to speak to anyone. He was fully within his rights to do so and it was her duty to comply.

Chapter 8

LIFE ON BOARD THE SHIP SETTLED into a rhythm. The lack of news was a bit disturbing as there were no newspapers each day to inform of the goings on in the world, nor any new information coming in. The ship was self-contained and it didn't take long to get to know the people traveling with them. Lysander had now met all of them. None of them were acquaintances he would normally keep and it was unlikely that he would at the end of the voyage, but some proved interesting company in the meantime. It was quite the fashion to keep interesting company, but Lysander had never been an ardent pursuer of tides of fashion.

Adele was more circumspect; she held to her own company more. Perhaps she was used to it, living in the country, and that was how she preferred it. He'd always assumed she preferred a quiet life; although all his assumptions about her went out the window since she crossed the world to conduct an illicit affair with a lieutenant. It seemed so out of character, but perhaps he'd never fully understood her character.

She'd been so quiet and demure—so colorless and purposeless. He knew that she attended church every Sunday without fail, as she'd done the one just passed. The chaplain on the ship had held service and she'd attended, no doubt praying over her sins—of which there actually were some grave ones. She was exactly the same as before, quiet, reserved and completely unengaging.

He would watch her as he came across her. While this was a handsome and large ship, there were only so many places one could go, and she seemed to prefer to sit on the promenade on the far side of the ship from their cabins. He wondered if she was trying to ignore him. Well, he'd found her hiding place—not that he was all that interested. His anger with her had dissipated somewhat now that he was back to deal with her—something he'd avoided as much as possible throughout their marriage. Perhaps because he knew she was unhappy. Her unhappiness would suck what little joy there was out of any room. They were both unhappy.

She sat reading most of the time, with a hat covering her face. She did look elegant—more so than he remembered. Surprisingly, his new acquaintances thought her charming—a bit aloof, but a fine woman. That had surprised him, because they were never qualities he'd seen. But perhaps their history had tainted his perception of her.

The past sat in his conscience, painfully demanding to be acknowledged. It was all tied to her—nothing to do with her and everything to do with her. He'd sold his soul for wealth and there had been a price.

*

He'd clenched his fist a thousand times on the walk over to the Sommerstock's house in Mayfair. He didn't normally walk, but this was a day he dreaded and he needed time to think. The bans were set to be announced in the paper tomorrow and he needed to tell her before she read it. There was a part of him that just wanted to leave it and not deal with the distress—a coward's way and he saw the appeal of it, but he wasn't a coward and he cared too much about her to let her find out through reading it along with everyone else.

But he'd left it to the last minute, hoping to find some way of avoiding this—of changing his father's mind. But all his father saw was the repair work required for their neglected properties; he was already planning the work and waiting for the dowry to come through.

Cassandra's house loomed in front of him. This was going to go badly. He wondered if he should consult with Ralph before—about how to break the news to his sister, but she deserved to be the first to know.

He knew Cassandra had expectations. Their romance had developed slowly—she being the sister of his best friend, Ralph, whom he'd met the first day of school and they had been inseparable ever since. They had the same circle of friends and they were jointly the center of that circle.

Cassandra had come along after her coming-out. She was dazzling and he'd been captured by her beauty and wit. She ruled the world and she knew it, fitting into their group perfectly, adding color and sparkle, and a sense of excitement they hadn't known they were missing.

She'd let him kiss her. They all attended events together and kept tight company to the envy of others. He'd loved being part of the group that everyone envied. It had been a magical time and all had been as it should have been.

Swallowing hard and clearing his throat, he knocked on the large, lacquered front door. As expected, the Sommerstock's butler gave him entrance and announced his arrival.

Cassandra, her mother and aunt were receiving and there was another woman present whom he didn't know. Briefly, he wondered whether he should retreat and come back another time, but he had left it so long, he didn't have any more time.

"Lysander! Lovely to see you," Cassandra's mother said. She'd always liked him and encouraged the friendship between him and her daughter. "Isn't it a wonderful day? This is Mrs. Wellers, an old friend of mine. This is Archie Warburton's son," she said to the other woman who appeared about the same age as Cassandra's mother.

"Ooo," Mrs. Wellers said. "I've known your father for a long time. Aren't you a handsome young man?"

Lysander would normally be quite happy to engage in this type of conversation with Mrs. Sommerstock and her acquaintances, but not today.

"I need to speak to Cassandra," he said nervously. They had been on a first name basis almost from the start.

Her mother considered him then exchanged glances with her daughter. A smile spread across her face. "Of course. Please, use the dining room." She pointed at the door to his left. He knew the dining room was there; he knew most of the house.

Cassandra rose and walked toward him, looking pleased and expectant, and he knew that the conversation she was expecting was different from the one she was about to have. As discussions in private were typically reserved for the most private of discussions, he suspected that the parties present expected that he would be proposing. He truly wished that was the case, but it wasn't. Instead, he was about to do something devastating.

Closing the sliding doors behind them, she turned to him, wearing a lilac-colored dress that went beautifully with her features, and was in the latest fashion. She always managed to dress in a way that was admired by others.

"I'm so glad to see you, Lys. You can't imagine how boring it is to sit through all these callers. Utterly dull—not an interesting thought between them. You will come to the Hallington event next week, won't you? It would be lovely to spend a few days in the country. I do need to get away from London for a while, with all the dramatics going on. Did you hear about Harriet and that Ralston man? Unbelievable. Who would have thought she had it in her?" She was chattering; she did when she was nervous.

He stood by the fireplace avoiding her eyes.

"What is it, Lys?" she asked, concern lacing her voice, knowing him well enough to perceive that something was wrong.

He didn't want to say it; he wanted to stay cordial—he wanted to stay at the point where a future for them was possible.

"Cassie," he started, his voice sounding gravelly. "Something has happened."

"What? Is anyone hurt?" She rushed over to him.

"No," he said and took her hand, feeling her warm, smooth skin under his fingers. He loved her. And he didn't want to do this, still unable to meet her eyes. "My father..." he started. He had to take a moment and form his words, and also to clear the lump he felt in his throat, "has made an agreement-"

"No, no, no," she started.

"I am to marry."

His world shook momentarily as she slapped him. A sharp ringing took over his hearing, but he knew he deserved it. Well, not him, his father, because this was his doing.

"No, you can't do this to me, Lys," she said and started pacing the room. "Lys, why have you done this?" There were tears in her voice; he could hear it even if he wasn't looking at her. Seeking her eyes, he saw they were as large as saucers.

"You know why," he said, defeated. The Sommerstocks had gravitas and respect, but not a great deal of wealth; nowhere near what the merchant Fowlers had. That was the difference between genteel and the trade class these days.

"Who is she?" Cassandra demanded.

"Just some girl. She's not important."

"And you'll marry her?"

"I have to."

"You don't have to," Cassandra said sharply.

"You know I will be disowned if I don't. I wish I could say that it didn't matter, but it does. You would never accept living in poverty. You weren't made for it."

Cassandra started pacing. They both knew it was true. They'd both been ruthless with acquaintances who lost their fortune and position. Being poor was worse than being diseased. If she was able to accept it, he would, but he knew that she would be miserable if they had to live in such reduced circumstances; losing their position in society and their prospects for the future. There was little recourse for a poor gentleman; they couldn't take employment, left to hope their family would take pity on them and leave them something in their will—ideally some wealthy childless aunt would leave them a decent-sized house, but those types of aunts were in short supply. Cassandra would hate that life and her bitterness would soon ruin their love. It would not be a life he'd enjoy either.

"I will always love you, Cassie."

Her tears made a sound as they dropped on the wooden floor. He heard the door slide sharply and Ralph stepped in, his mother following, looking concerned. She rushed over to her daughter and put her arms around her.

"Get out of here, Lys," Ralph demanded. The harsh look on his face spelled that he wasn't welcome anymore. He wanted to explain, but he was smartly shown out to the street by the butler and the door closed behind him.

*

Lysander watched the reading woman who was leaning slightly to her side to avoid the sun that was encroaching on her spot.

None of his friends had attended his wedding. He'd understood their reticence, but it had proven permanent. He'd lost his whole group of acquaintances, being judged by them as grasping and uncouth, marrying into the lower classes to improve his position. The desertion of Ralph had hurt the most and it had proved even longer than Cassandra's anger. Cassandra hadn't spoken to him for a whole year, although she had eventually forgiven him, or said as much, but while Ralph was polite and cordial, their familiarity was a thing of the past.

Harry had only been a peripheral friend at the time, but he was the only one who'd stuck by him and they had become true friends since. Loyalty turned out to be a most admirable quality, Lysander had learnt, and Harry had it no matter what happened.

Lysander had become content with his life, but he sometimes wondered what his life would be like if he'd married Cassandra, particularly if his father had seen Cassandra as a suitable bride, which she was—but his father had been distracted by their diminishing wealth. Lysander was not the only person by far to marry into wealthy families of lower classes; it was a common occurrence, but there was an ongoing stigma attached.

None of this was technically Adele's fault, but he'd been too angry at the time to see that, and perhaps too young. He'd blamed her for all of it and he'd never warmed to her. The results of their joining stared him in the face even as the fortunes of his former friends suffered, while his family remained strong and wealthy due to the fresh infusion of funds that the Fowler family had afforded them. Wealth wasn't everything, although he often tried to convince himself that it was of upmost importance, but in his heart, knew it wasn't. Maybe that was something she'd discovered in her Lieutenant. A flash of anger shot through him, but he neither fed it nor analyzed it.

Chapter 9

ADELE STAYED IN HER CABIN during the mornings, where tea, eggs and bread were brought to her. She'd join Lysander at lunch, when they would dine in the salon, then again at supper time. Otherwise, they spent no time together. Late in the morning, she would find her table and chair on the shaded side of the ship and read, while in the afternoons she rested. Her life in Adelaide required much more activity; managing the children, then making her way home to eat supper with the girls in her boarding house.

But here the weeks seemed to flow by, even though she did very little during the days. Having a routine helped, she knew. If nothing else, there was routine to adhere to.

It took some adjustment to consider herself Lady Warburton again, let alone Lysander's wife. In truth, she'd never spent this much time with him throughout their marriage. Still, she felt less married than she had before. There was a vast amount of things that had happened to her since she'd considered herself his wife.

He'd apologized to her, which was something he'd never done before—for anything. She'd spent a great deal of time wondering what had gone through his mind when he'd found her. He'd trespassed on her person and she wondered if he hated her. His actions seemed to indicate that he did, but then he had apologized. In her recollection, he hadn't shown much of any emotion since, not even the distaste and dismissal she was presented with before she'd left him.

"There you are, my dear," Mrs. Callisfore said one late morning as she sat on the promenade and read. Mrs. Callisfore placed her bulk heavily down in the chair, while placing her cane to lean against her knee. "My knees fare better in the heat, but they are still trying. If there is one thing I could recommend, it is to never grow old."

"I wish I could promise you that, Mrs. Callisfore, but I'm afraid I haven't found the means to avert it," Adele said kindly.

"I suppose it's better than being dead," the woman said and rested her hand on the edge of the table. "Where is that handsome husband of yours?"

Adele wasn't entirely sure. "I believe he is reading in the smoking room."

"Ah, the gentleman's retreat. I wanted to invite him, both of you, to a reading tomorrow night. Mrs. Fullfer is reading her translation of ancient Persian poetry tomorrow night. Strange woman. What manner of woman is fluent in ancient Persian? I'll never understand. But I thought your husband might find it interesting."

"I'm sure he will," Adele said with a measured smile, not entirely sure if her husband would be interested in ancient Persian poetry, but she knew he liked to do things in the evenings. She would retreat to her cabin after supper and he would sometimes attend various activities on the ship. Listening through the walls as she lay in bed, she'd hear him return in the evenings.

"A fine man, your husband. You must be a lucky creature to be the wife of such a man—and titled, too."

Adele smiled again, still astounded that people couldn't see the dire and unenviable state of their marriage. Looking down, she twisted a handkerchief in her lap, not sure what this woman would think of her husband if she knew that the only time he touched her was when he'd almost forced himself on her in a state of rage after finding her hiding on the other side of the world. Obviously, she would never mention it; it wasn't a true account of his character. It was known that there were violent and unreasonable husbands

73

from which women had to flee. Lysander wasn't one of those. The only time she'd seen any temper on him at all was when he'd first found her in Adelaide. Instead, she smiled. "I will remember to tell him."

Mrs. Callisfore nodded her appreciation and groaned as she rose from the chair. "This is a nice spot," she said. "I will join you in a moment of quiet reading one day, but today I've been invited to tea with that woman from Dover." Adele nodded her understanding and Mrs. Callisfore slowly moved away, leaning heavily on her walking cane.

Placing a marker in her book, Adele decided to deliver the message she'd been commissioned with before it slipped her mind. Lysander was probably away from his cabin and it would be a good time to leave him a note.

Arriving back in her own cabin, she placed her things on a table, before testing the handle of his door and it opened without effort. His room was similar in size to hers, but it had a more masculine decor. These cabins were obviously built for a married couple, with one decorated for a female and the other for a man. His furniture was heavier and darker, giving the room a very different feel from her own.

His scent lingered in the room. This was his domain. Everything was neatly placed. He'd always seemed to hold a preference for neatness. She'd kept the Devon house in the same neat order—not that he saw it or her efforts the vast majority of time.

She felt uncomfortable being in his room—his space—as if she was intruding. Stepping over to the bed, she saw a book on the side bed. He must be reading it in the evenings as he took to bed. Reading the gold leaf printed title down the spine, she saw it was a book on arctic exploration in the far Northern Russia. Not exactly a book she'd expected to see, but then she didn't really know what to expect. It only went to show how little she knew him, and knowing him was something she'd strived for once upon a time.

*

Adele entered the room he still occupied when in residence. It was the same room he'd used all his life, and it still had some things from his childhood—a sailboat that he must have used on the lake. The boat was beautifully crafted with replica rigging and gear. She'd seen it a hundred times and it was a shame that there wasn't a child to be delighted with it. She'd never seen Lysander bring it out, so she wondered why he kept it.

Perhaps he kept it for his own son, but that couldn't be on his mind as he never touched her in a way that would result in a child. He never touched her at all. The only time he'd touched her since their wedding night was when he assisted her out of a carriage, which he did strictly out of duty. He was required to assist any female out of a carriage, known or unknown—even his wife.

Walking into his bedroom, her steps echoed on the floorboards until she reached carpet. She noticed a hint of mustiness and told herself that she needed to remind the housekeeper to air the Master's room.

His effects were neatly displayed in a row. There were a comb, a nail brush and a razor hidden in an ivory case. She ran her fingers over the masculine items, feeling the textures of the cold metal, swine hair and smooth tortoise-shell under her fingers.

This room smelled of him—the merest hint, but she knew the smell well. She'd been in this room more times than she could count; to check everything was in order, but also, this was where she felt his presence. It was different from any other room in the house. It had secrets and meaning, and she was still trying to unravel them.

She knew each book in this room and she'd even read some of them, but she had no idea when he'd read them or what his interests had been at the time. He probably wasn't aware they were here anymore, a reflection of some past interest of his, put aside and forgotten.

*

"What are you doing here?" His voice broke through her reminiscing. Reacting with a start, she turned to face him. She hadn't heard him enter. He placed his hat on one of the side tables.

"I am here to leave you a note, but since you are here: Mrs. Callisfore wishes to invite you to a reading of ancient Persian poetry being presented by Mrs. Fullfer." Her voice was strong and crisp, and she congratulated herself for not blushing and cowering at being caught in his cabin. She still had trouble holding his eyes, feeling a strong urge to look away from his blue, piercing eyes.

"The writing desk is over here," he said, pointing to the other side of the room. Suspicion laced his eyes. She was effectively on the wrong side of the cabin, where she wouldn't be if her intention was to write a note. Which was her intention! She'd just gotten distracted.

"It is interesting to note that they've planned different decor for the male and female passengers." It was the only excuse she could think of. It sounded weak, but there was nothing else she could say.

Leaning back on the side table, he crossed his arms and considered her. "Yes, they have been particular in their detail."

Silence prevailed, stretching uncomfortably. It was one of the few times they were alone as their typical association was in the salon or on the way there.

"What are your plans when we return?" she finally asked. The thought had plagued her and she didn't often get moments in private in which to ask.

Looking down, he crossed his ankles as well and looked out the porthole. "Did Mrs. Callisfore invite me or did she invite us both?"

"Technically the invitation was for the both of us," she admitted. She wanted to lie, but she didn't feel comfortable lying to him, which was paradoxical considering she had conducted such a grave ruse about her own demise.

"Then we shall both attend."

Looking down at the floor, she nodded. She didn't usually attend any evening activities, and she wasn't entirely sure why he wanted her to join him. It didn't go unnoticed that he didn't answer her question. Perhaps he was trying to punish her by keeping her fate unknown to her. She wasn't entirely sure it mattered; she had no power in this situation, having to comply with whatever he wanted, which was her duty—what she'd swore to do when she'd given her vows, and it was the law for that matter. She was his to do with as he pleased and if he wished to punish her by keeping her ignorant of his intentions, then it was his choice. She didn't even have a moral right to wish better treatment from him.

"As you wish," she said and retreated back to the connecting door between their cabins. Closing the door behind her, she leant on it and closed her eyes, unsure if she would be more comfortable if he was angry with her, but they were back to nothingness. But then perhaps he just hid his anger well.

He wanted her to accompany him to the poetry reading. He was still presenting her as his wife; as a united couple with no indication of their true state. Maybe he was trying to show her the things he would deprive her of when they returned. She didn't know what she preferred, but she suspected it would be uncomfortable whichever way he chose to handle this.

Chapter 10

WAITING FOR HER TO EMERGE from her cabin, he noticed the gentle movement and remembered that he was on a ship. It was so stable most of the time, he'd sometimes forget. Impatience nipped at his heels as he waited, but he wouldn't rush her. The woman's toilette was a thing of mystery—something for men to be unaware of.

He'd learnt her routine now, and he knew where she was most of the time, ensuring he went out of his way to avoid her. He wasn't afraid of a confrontation as such, although he didn't think she'd make a scene—unlike Evie, who would be in full dramatics. Evie liked dramatics; she was animated and full of life, and it had been what had drawn him to her. But she could also be trying, because sometimes he got the feeling that it was more about the dramatics for Evie than the purpose for them. It grew tiring. He went long stretches without seeing her, which only increased the probability and nature of the dramatics—putting him off seeing her for even longer stretches. But eventually, his needs outweighed the unpleasantness. She'd been his mistress for three years now, but he'd started thinking about the idea of letting her go and finding another—a task he'd never gotten around to. He certainly didn't understand the men who changed their mistresses each month—just the sheer unpleasantness involved put him off.

Finally, Adele emerged from her room, wearing the yellow gown he'd seen quite a few times now. "Have you nothing else to wear?"

"No, I don't." She looked at him and he wondered if he saw defiance there. It wasn't blatant, but he suspected he saw flashes of it. "My wardrobe was minimized with other purposes in mind."

Lysander frowned. It was unfortunate as he'd already sent her effects from India home—keeping one's wife in one gown was untenable for a man in his position, but then there was nothing for it. He couldn't very well have a new wardrobe made in the middle of the ocean. Or maybe he could; he should enquire, he told himself. Money did tend to solve any problem.

Holding out his arm, she took it as they started walking toward the salon. She kept her hair simple, perhaps too simple for the fashion, but it did suit her. It had a certain elegance to it—elegance he'd never noticed in her before.

Perhaps the trying nature of his voyage and the inherent dramatics of finding his wife halfway across the globe, was having a strange effect on him. All of a sudden, he was finding his demure and tedious wife elegant.

They were directed to the room where the poetry reading was being held. Mrs. Fullfer was standing at the front, graciously awaiting her start, smiling broadly with her head held high, looking slightly nervous, but adoring being the center of attention.

With her hand, Mrs. Callisfore patted the two spare seats next to her, indicating they should join her. Such a direct invitation couldn't be ignored and Adele walked into the row ahead of Lysander, to take the seat next to the elderly woman.

"You look lovely this evening," Mrs. Callisfore said and they exchanged pleasantries. "It seems Mrs. Fullfer is about to have the moment she has been preparing for. She lives in Brighton with her brother, did you know? Says the sea is soothing for her artistic temperament. There might be something to it. Perhaps some of our sanitariums should be moved to the seaside."

Patiently, Lysander diverted his eyes elsewhere and ignored the statement. Mrs. Callisfore could be cantankerous at times, as seemed to be the assumed right of ladies of her years in relation to women of similarly advanced age.

He watched as people entered the room. There was the American couple, the Australian politician and his wife, the steam-boiler merchant and lastly the professor from New York. He knew all the persons traveling with them now— more than he'd ever wanted to, but it seemed to be the nature of these things. The distances between classes and peoples were thin or non-existent. He didn't truly mind; he wasn't a complete snob, but he also knew that the camaraderie that was felt in circumstances like this didn't last once they'd reached port.

He noted that Adele's eyes followed the American professor, in his brown suit—one that offended Lysander in both its inelegance and inappropriateness for the occasion. But some Americans, particularly the men, didn't seem to prescribe or understand the requirements for dress for certain occasions. The disturbing idea of what Adele saw in the American man entered his mind. He'd instantly assumed that she would see the same thing as him, but then she'd run off with a lowly lieutenant, cavorting across half the world. Perhaps it wasn't the inappropriate attire she saw, but the strong jawline, the sprinkling of gray hair at his temples and the beaming smile as he took his seat and greeted his companion.

Lysander watched his wife; saw where her gaze traveled. For all he knew, she could be looking for her next conquest. His mind traveled back to the room where she and her companion had lived in India, the large bed, where they'd slept. Likely where she'd given herself wantonly.

Looking down at his lap, he felt anger flare in him, at the inappropriateness of it all. Perhaps there were inappropriate thoughts in her when she looked at men like the American professor. He would never call it jealousy, but something raged in him at the thought. Beneath her prim and demure mask, there might well be someone manipulative and grasping.

"Have you ever traveled to Egypt?" Mrs. Callisfore asked. He knew the question was directed to him, but he didn't feel calm enough to answer at the moment. Keeping his face turned in the other direction, he forced himself to be calm, even if he didn't really want to.

"No, but I had an uncle who went a few years back, and he adored it," Adele interceded, distracting and directing attention away from his rudeness. Lysander snapped his eyes back to her and watched as she conveyed her uncle's anecdotes. Now she was acting the appropriate and conscientious wife. She couldn't be both saint and harlot, but she was acting both.

She'd wanted to know what he was going to do with her when they returned. He hadn't answered. He didn't know the answer. It was a question he'd been ignoring.

Mrs. Fullfer started reading, pronunciating each word in a melodramatically somber voice. She would intermittently speed up and slow down for dramatic effect, her voice too loud and disturbing to sleep through, Lysander determined, but he closed his eyes and cursed himself for agreeing to come to this evening. He wasn't entirely sure why he had, maybe because Adele had tried to gloss over the fact that they'd been invited as a couple.

Intermission finally came around.

"I am parched," Mrs. Callisfore said. "Be a darling, my lord, and fetch us some glasses of punch." It was an order and he had to comply, being at the mercy of matrons—

irrespective of his position, he took orders from the matrons of society. Mrs. Callisfore would likely order the Pope around if he were present. Strictly, Lysander didn't mind, but it did sometimes amuse him how the fairer sex really had men under their thumbs, and if anyone thought otherwise, they were fools.

A table had been set up in the back, with a large crystal punch bowl. A server stood behind it wearing white gloves, waiting to provide assistance. As Lysander only had two hands, he would bring two glasses for the women and forego one for himself—which was fine as punch was often too sweet for his tastes.

When he returned with two glasses in his hands, the American professor was speaking animatedly to the women, his eyes on Adele. A frown crossed Lysander's brow and he wondered again what Adele saw when he looked at the man, receiving his attention. She was listening intently to what the man was saying.

"Ah, Lord Warburton, you brought punch, you darling." Suddenly, he felt ridiculous standing there with two dainty glasses in his hands—a look which he could well imagine didn't portray a great degree of masculinity. "This is Professor Smith; he has been telling us of the geology of Australia. Fascinating. Are you a Darwinian?"

"No," he said. He was, in principle, but for some reason, he felt like being obtuse. Adele turned her surprised gaze to him, before hiding it with a smile. She was playing the part of a wife, who would be fully cognizant of her husband's beliefs and views.

The women received the glasses and he felt better being relieved of the emasculating burden.

"Are you a geologist, Professor Smith?" he asked.

"I am, sir."

"He travels the world looking for interesting rock formations. Can you imagine?" Mrs. Callisfore said.

Lysander smiled tightly, finding the man extremely annoying, addressing him by the wrong title and the way the man's eyes lingered on his wife—he couldn't help but notice it. This man, with his gentle puppy-dog eyes—deceptive in their portrayal, was probably thinking lewd thoughts about his wife, while smiling congenially. An adventurer, an explorer, a man set on uncovering secrets and unknown ideas—the kind of man who women celebrated. Lysander, with his regimented life, surrounded by luxury and exacting standards, might be thought by some—when measured against the criteria of setting the imagination aflutter—to pale in comparison.

Lysander hated feeling inadequate. He watched as Adele listened to the American, with his broad and mellow accent, wondering if she found him charming. She had in the past found Samson Ellingwood charming, enough to abandon her station and run off with him, with all the man's relative disadvantages, that had offered even less when you considered his quick death. It seemed illogical, but it only proved that he didn't understand this woman well; he'd thought he had, but she was something other than what he'd thought. And men like this professor, found her charming, he thought with vexation. The wife whom he'd seen as exciting as a dishcloth was thought charming by others— charming enough that Samson Ellingwood would limit his prospects to be with her.

He couldn't have her cuckolding him again, particularly here in closed confines, where everyone would notice. He would have to guard to ensure that she wasn't succumbing to this American man's charms, and he needed to say something about it—make sure she understood that such behavior wouldn't be tolerated, but it was an

83

uncomfortable discussion—one that may open the door to more than he intended. A further bell indicated that Mrs. Fullfer was ready to start again.

"I believe I am coming down with a headache," Adele said. "I think I shall have to retreat to my cabin."

"Of course, dear," Mrs. Callisfore said, patting her hand. "You must go lie down—rest until you feel better."

Adele bid goodbye to Mrs. Callisfore, and to the professor, who bowed to her, taking her hand in a slight touch. Lysander wondered if her gaze lingered a little longer on the man than was necessary.

"I will walk you back," Lysander stated.

"It is alright; you stay. I know the way."

"I will all the same."

"As you please."

As they walked out of the salon onto the exterior promenade, the brisk sea air was strong that evening, and it was pitch black away from the deck, as if they were on a ship in the middle of nothingness.

Lysander envied women's ability to claim headaches anytime they wanted, and were excused. Men couldn't claim a headache even if they were dying of typhoid. Because of this, he had to go back and sit through the torture of Mrs. Fulfer's recital until the bitter end.

Feeling the uncomfortable silence between himself and the woman walking next to him, his wife, he wished there was some conversation they could embark on, but the truth was that he had more to say to a stranger. Light banter seemed disingenuous considering the chasm between them—a chasm filled with a large wasp nest, for which any attempt at discourse would only serve as a swift kick, sending all their crimes and recriminations into the open.

Lysander wasn't stupid enough not to realize that he wasn't an entirely innocent party in this mess. He couldn't entirely claim victimhood there, because his inadequacies may well have contributed to the strained affairs between himself and his wife—another topic he wasn't relishing dragging into the light.

"I think there are some things we need to discuss," he said as they reached her cabin.

Adele agreed wholeheartedly, biting her cheek on the inside as she tried to think of how to broach the subject, but couldn't think of any clever ways. "What are you to do with me when we return?" she demanded.

He considered her for a moment, his eyes dark and unyielding, but he stepped over to open his cabin door, giving her room to proceed before him. The smell of him enveloped her, automatically recalling the excitement she used to feel when she caught his scent from his things abandoned in the Devon house—just like he'd done her.

His head shifted back slightly and he looked annoyed. He had no right to be annoyed, she felt, anger unfolding in her, which she quickly suppressed.

He wasn't answering. "Are you being deliberately cruel by not telling me?"

"You would deserve it if I was," he said, his voice low and coarse. She wondered if he was affected by drink, but there were no visible signs.

"Are you?"

Turning from her, he placed a program he'd been holding on the dressing table. "No," he said after a lengthy pause. "I don't know. The true answer is: I don't know what to do with you."

It was the first honest answer he'd ever given her, but it put her no closer to knowing what her future held. Still, it was something.

"What do you think I should do with you?" he asked, looked back at her. "An untrue wife. An adulteress."

"Oh please," she said with anger. She'd never before been angry with him present, but she couldn't hold it back now; it came flowing out of her. "You cannot claim that my lack of fidelity is what aggrieves you—you have been living with a woman for years. What is her name, Miss Hamilton, I believe?" She could see the muscles of his jaw working with displeasure and anger. He might not like hearing it, but it was true. "I spent years being loyal to you, preserving my chastity like a sacred gift belonging to you—it wasn't something you appreciated."

"Perhaps, my dear, it is your lack of discretion that offends. Or are you completely oblivious of the embarrassment that you have caused me, my family—not to mention your own."

"My own family? Are you unaware that I have none left?"

"You still need to honor your family name, as you needed to honor my name. You've made me the laughing stock of London. The burden of you is never-ending."

"If I am such a burden, I wonder why you felt the need to cross the world to retrieve me? You could have left me where I was."

"Because we cannot just shake off our burdens—that is not our right." He was speaking in sharp, angry tones. She hadn't meant for the conversation to go this way, but perhaps there was no other way for it to go. "You can't just shake it off like a coat and leave it behind. It doesn't work that way. You swore an oath and you will keep to it."

"And I did, for years, but you placed me in a position I could not bear. I was suffocating—dying."

"Don't be melodramatic," he said with distaste.

She went silent with anger, watching him. She couldn't trust herself to speak, she was so angry with him for completely dismissing the suffering she'd gone through. "I

86

want a divorce," she said icily, feeling as though anger was dripping off her. "You care nothing for my happiness."

"No," he said, simply and decisively.

Adele thought for a moment he was agreeing that he didn't care for her happiness, but it sunk in that he said no to the divorce. Adele stared at him in disbelief, trying to think of some reason for why he would refuse her at this point— when they'd gone years without ever managing to even stay in the same room. "You have every reason in the world—no one would argue the grounds. I wouldn't even challenge it—I'm even begging you."

"I will not discuss this further, but while we are speaking frankly, there is an issue I need to address with you." His sharp eyes were boring into her. "I will not have you touting your charms with men on this ship."

Adele gasped at the blatant accusation, which was underserved. She recalled how he'd called her a whore at one point, and was now accusing her of receiving the attention of other men. Reaching back, she slapped him hard across the face.

Grabbing her wrist, he forced it around her back, which brought her body into full contact with his. His grip was painful on her wrist and he looked down on her forbiddingly as he held her in place. As she whimpered with the pain, he let her go and stepped away. There was complete silence in the room as she stared at him, trying to understand where they stood in relation to each other. "You bring out the very worst in me," he said. "You always have. I swear, you bring me to depths I didn't know I had, and never wanted to know." Lysander turned his back on her. "You are overwrought and have given yourself over to dramatics. You should withdraw to your room."

"Do not treat me like a child," she warned.

"Then stop acting like one."

"You're despicable."

"Then it is a description that can be attributed to both of us."

"I found a man who cared about me, who loved me. In the short time I was with him, he was a better husband than you ever were."

"But the point is that he wasn't your husband, Lady Warburton. There is a significant point of distinction."

Marching out of his room, Adele slammed the door, feeling herself shaking with anger and resentment. She was married to an absolutely impossible man—he always had been, so she wasn't sure why she was surprised.

Chapter 11

LYSANDER DIDN'T SPEAK with Adele after that incident when she'd come into his cabin, accusing him. In truth, she hadn't spoken to him either. They carried on as they had been, dining together; him walking her to the salon and then back to her cabin at the end of the evening, but they didn't speak beyond the necessary practicalities. Her distance from him was a little more pronounced, almost as if she was a little unsure of him. He couldn't entirely blame her; he'd behaved atrociously and he wasn't proud of it. She just drove him to distraction and he reacted to it, which he shouldn't. He had to reassert proper control of himself. This was not the person he wanted to be. Perhaps it was a good idea, decreasing the contact and increasing the distance between them.

Sitting at the table in the salon, he watched the mingling that evening. His wife was discussing something with an Australian widow, returning to England to live with her sister, his wife tall in comparison and he noted other people saw her as compelling and handsome—not the gawky girl with huge eyes he always saw in his mind's eye when he thought of her. He realized that when he thought of her, he saw her as she had been and she clearly wasn't that creature anymore.

Men found her attractive, and while he'd gotten used to the idea, it still annoyed him when men spoke to her, particularly the professor as he suspected Adele enjoyed his company. Another man had uncovered the passion in the woman who was his wife, having taken her from girlhood to womanhood, and it had happened while he hadn't been paying attention. But perhaps that was the point: he hadn't been paying attention and he'd left her unguarded for other men to find.

The most uncomfortable aftermath of their row some nights back was the knowledge that her desertion of their marriage hadn't been entirely about her being swayed by other men or her being driven by a defective character, but driven, to some degree, by her dissatisfaction with their marriage. It was an uncomfortable idea, because it brought the culpability swinging back in his direction.

He wasn't cowardly in the sense that he refused to accept his own responsibility in matters. He knew he'd been a terrible husband and on some level he accepted that his wife's desertion was in some ways justified—morally, in some respects, if not legally.

As he watched, the American geologist approached her and she smiled. Frowning, Lysander realized that she never smiled when he approached her. Clearly, his wife hated him. It was not an uncommon state in marriage; he knew few people whose marriages were actually successful. Marriage wasn't about success; it was about stability, family and securing the future—consolidating position. He had grown to accept his father's take on the institution over time—looking past his youthful naivety.

Taking a swig of his drink, he winced as the liquid burnt the back of his throat, numbing slightly as it went. He didn't usually drink this make of whiskey, but for some reason, he desired the burn it always gave him. He still didn't know what to do about his marriage. She'd asked for a divorce and he'd refused, but his adamant refusal had actually been a reflection of his anger; he'd been spiteful when he'd refused her proposal. He wasn't proud of his spiteful reaction, but on the other hand, he did believe everything he'd said: marriage was a duty one could not just cast aside; it wasn't about happiness, it was about duty. But his marriage had also caused him a great degree of embarrassment and would continue to do so. His reputation had been truly damaged by his inconstant wife and accepting her back would be perceived as weak character by the men in his acquaintance.

As he watched, Adele accepted a drink from the waiter. It didn't take long for someone to spot that she was alone and started engaging her in conversation. A few months back, he'd have expected her to be hiding along the edge of the room, where no-one noticed her—that had been his understanding of his wife. In his absence, his wife had become a delightful woman.

*

Adele took a seat by her husband, smoothing out the creases in her second-best dress. It wasn't really of sufficient quality for the surroundings, but she couldn't wear the yellow dress all the time; it'd be threadbare before she reached London. She had little choice but to utilize some of the dresses she wore as a schoolmistress, unsuitable as they were.

Sitting next to her, Lysander spoke to the American banker—a man she knew he actually liked conversing with. The American banker, who was traveling the world with his wife, had many interesting topics of conversation, which Lysander had an appreciation for. She watched his face as they spoke, noticing the lines that were starting to encroach on his features. His eyes moved as he thought about the things he was being told. He was intelligent, she could see that now, having never actually spent enough time with him to know with any certainty. This was what he looked like when he was interested in something—not usually the look she received, where his face would be much more tightly drawn when he looked at her and she could sometimes see suspicion in his eyes, as if he didn't trust her.

"You must give it a turn," Mrs. Callisfore addressed her from further down the table. "It pleases us older persons to see a handsome couple dancing."

"Dancing?" Adele repeated with a moment of panic. Not only had she been caught in a moment of absent contemplation, but also in a context with dancing involved. Her eyes shot to Lysander.

"The dancing is about to start."

Adele turned back to Mrs. Callisfore. "I'm not sure I should…" she drifted off, again returning her gaze to Lysander who coolly regarded her. Adele had actually been hoping to return to her cabin early like she did most nights. She wasn't sure, but she wondered if she saw accusation in his eyes, exactly like he used to on the rare occasion they were together, when he'd felt she was tedious and dull.

The accusation of their argument still hung in the air between them. Nothing had been resolved, but they both now knew the depth of their regard for one another.

"Come now," Mrs. Callisfore pushed. "I am sure your Lord Warburton would love to twirl you around on the dance floor, my dear. It would be such a handsome sight."

Looking down, Adele felt Lysander's accusation sting. As much as she wanted to escape his judgment, she couldn't quite achieve it. And it was an unfair accusation, especially coming from him. Looking him squarely in the eyes, she held her head high. "If Lord Warburton would be so inclined, I would of course dance with him."

He turned his head slightly at the challenge. She'd never directly challenged him in public like that before—almost like she was challenging his perception of her. "As you wish, my dear."

The endearment felt goading. He only did it in public, to keep up appearances, but it seemed that they were having a display of wills tonight and Adele was wondering if this was a good idea. She remained quiet for a while, until the dancing started. Everyone knew of their indication to dance and were watching them expectantly when it started.

Lysander rose and approached her, looking exactly as arrogant and forbidding as he always did. Holding out his hand, he expected her to take it. Something in her warned against doing so, as if she needed to protect herself from whatever this would intimate. Guardedly, her eyes sought out his again. The accusation was still there, even as she placed her fingers in his warm hand.

She rose as he gently pulled her up out of her seat and led her to the center of the floor where the dancing had started. Waltzing, of course. Turning to her, his hand repositioned to hers, bringing them palm to palm. She never touched his skin and the feel was confronting; the touch radiating out through her arm, making her tingle. His other hand moved around her back, settling at its base, warm and firm. His mouth was close to her eyes, forcing her to see him much more intimately than she could remember seeing. This dance alluded to intimacy without allowing the full contact between their bodies. This was definitely not a good idea.

Lysander started moving, forcing Adele to follow his lead and to place her hand on his shoulder. In this dance, she had to follow him, just like she had to in real life. This elegant dance also highlighted the true nature of control in relationships between men and women—the control he had over her—as if to say beautiful things happened when there was harmony between them.

Adele felt short of breath as he turned her around on the floor, more so when their thighs would touch as they moved. It was intensely uncomfortable, but she had to bear this as she had so completely risen to the challenge he'd presented, while resenting herself for still caring.

Mercifully the dance ended and Adele was finally released from the embrace. He had strictly kept the required space between their bodies throughout the dance, but it was unnerving nonetheless.

Returning to the table, Lysander turned to her. "Do you wish to return to your cabin?"

"No, I'm fine," she lied. She really did want to return, but his goading still drove her.

Considering her for a moment, he then nodded and turned to participate in a discussion as they neared a group. Adele still felt assaulted and confronted by their recent physical intimacy. Slowly, she drifted toward the conversation as well.

"Would you care to dance once more?" Professor Smith asked her. Again, she felt a moment of panic, but for different reasons. "If your husband wouldn't mind, of course."

Lysander looked tense with the muscles of his jaw twinging, but he nodded graciously.

Adele took the professor's hand, but it didn't have the charged feeling that it had with Lysander. The professor led her to the floor and twirled her to him. Lysander's accusation that she encouraged the attention of other men flitted through her mind. On one level it was true; she preferred the attention of other men over her husband; dancing with the professor was more fun than challenging. There wasn't the heavy bearing of meaning that it had with her husband. This dance was just for the sheer joy of it and she smiled as he started turning her around, conscious that Lysander's eyes were on her. She actually did enjoy dancing normally, and the enjoyment of it seemed to be returning, and it ended much too quickly, returning her to the solemn and disapproving countenance of her husband. Lysander nodded tightly as the professor returned her to Lysander's care. Adele almost regretted it; for a moment, she had been away from the gravity of their dealings, for a moment of carefree and light enjoyment.

"You are proving quite a popular dance partner tonight," he said.

"So it would appear," she said guardedly.

"I think it is time to retire. The evening grows late and I know how much you dislike staying up."

A frown fleeted across her face. Lysander didn't normally direct her comings and goings, but he was tonight, knowing it had to do with the professor dancing with her.

"I will escort you," he said.

"Thank you." She didn't mind withdrawing. The evening had been tense and uncomfortable. Lysander's presence at her side had been impossible to ignore. Escaping would be merciful, even if being told to do so grated, but being away from his scrutiny made his overbearingness worth suffering.

The night was clearly humid and she would sleep badly that night, even with the more rigorous exercise that evening. She would toss and turn, trying to alleviate the ill-at-ease feeling brought on by this weather. But she knew it was more than weather. The fact that they had departed Australia and were now firmly on their way to Europe only brought home the idea that she was returning to London and the life she'd lived before—the one she couldn't tolerate.

Chapter 12

ADELE TOOK HER USUAL seat on the shady side of the ship, where she preferred to spend her days. Everyone knew where to find her and now that she knew well the people traveling with them, she didn't mind so much when people stopped to chat as they took their exercise or wiled away their boredom. She knew the circumstances and intentions of everyone on the ship.

"It appears we will part company soon," Mrs. Callisfore said, sitting down in the other chair.

"We will?" Adele said with confusion.

"It is only a few days until we reach the Suez and I will be continuing on to Jerusalem, I have decided. I thought it would be a shame to pass this way and not stop by. Have you ever been?" Adele shook her head. "You should make that handsome husband take you."

Smiling tightly as had become customary at the mention of her husband, Adele ran her gloved finger along the spine of the book she'd put aside. Mr. Ellingwood was the kind of man who would be happy to stop somewhere to just explore, but that was not her situation now. "I am not sure the heat agrees with Lord Warburton."

"What are your plans, dear?"

Adele realized that she had absolutely no idea. She hadn't even realized they were going through the Suez, or that they were so close to it.

"I am not sure. Lord Warburton does all the planning."

Mrs. Callisfore reached over and patted her hand. "I do hope you will come see me sometime. You are such a lovely girl and I would very much like our acquaintance to continue."

"Of course," Adele said with a more genuine smile. Visiting Mrs. Callisfore was one thing she could plan for her future. Surely Lysander wouldn't refuse her request. Feeling her smile slip a bit, she forced it back. She was to stay married to him; he'd refused her a divorce. "That would be lovely."

"I suppose this ship will return to Australia now," Mrs. Callisfore said.

Adele hadn't known the ship wouldn't continue. She had to ask Lysander to tell her what their plans were. This ship apparently wasn't taking them all the way to England, but would be returning. Leaning back, she contemplated the idea of returning to Australia with the ship, but she knew Lysander wouldn't allow it. Misery bit at her heels, but she refused to give into it. She was going back to London and if lucky enough to find someone who cared for her again; she would just have to take Lysander's suggestion and find her happiness with more discretion. It hadn't actually been a recommendation of his, but she couldn't continue like she had been. If there was one thing she'd learnt it was that she was responsible for her own happiness.

*

Adele took Lysander's arm as he walked her to the salon to dine that evening, a habit they had done in silence more times than she could count.

"We will be traveling through the canal soon," she stated. "Will we travel straight to England from there?"

"No, we will disembark in Venice, from where we will continue north by rail."

"Oh," she said, realizing that they would be in Europe very shortly.

She wanted to beg him to let her return to Australia with this ship, but she already knew what the answer would be, and her question could very well invite a further candid revelation of their feelings. She saw no purpose in it; she'd revealed her feelings in sufficient detail last time, and the truth was that he didn't care. He'd been perfectly clear when he'd said his concerns were exclusively for duty.

"How long will we stay in Venice?" As distressing as the thought of Europe was, the idea of seeing Venice was exciting. It was one of the places she'd always wanted to see—one of the unique places on earth with a convergence of history, culture and beauty.

"We are leaving as soon as we arrive."

"But it is Venice, aren't you curious to see the city?"

"In all honesty, this was never meant to be a trip to explore European cities; I went to retrieve the effects of my deceased wife. I am not about to go gallivanting around an Italian city."

Closing her mouth, Adele looked away, wondering if he would highlight her crimes from now on in response to every request she put to him. Any ounce of joy and excitement and he sucked it out of the air. "Of course," she said, letting go of his arm, feeling as if she needed some distance. There were times when it was simply too hard to even act the part of dutiful wife.

Ensuring to smile broadly, she entered the salon. It was time to perform—a duty ingrained in her from earliest girlhood. She wondered at the idea of not doing it; of refusing to act the part and admit to all of these people here that not only was her marriage in an atrocious state, she'd run away from her husband and he was now returning her to the prison he kept her in. She could well imagine the shocked faces of the people present—probably more so for the honest confession over the reality of her situation. Honesty was not done—one did not wash one's own dirty linen in public, no matter how bad the true situation was. One never admitted dislike or discord with anyone, particularly not one's husband. These things were borne with grace.

Chapter 13

THEY'D CHANGED SHIPS IN the Port of Tawfiq, just at the Red Sea entrance to the Suez, having said goodbye to some of their acquaintances from the steamship; people Lysander had grown used to seeing every day over the last few months. Adele had said a fond goodbye to some of the friends she'd made on the trip, particularly Mrs. Callisfore, who had made Lysander promise to send Adele to see her when they were back in England. The woman was skilled at putting things in a way that he couldn't refuse, so he'd had to say 'Of course, at Lady Warburton's opportunity.'

They had transferred to the other ship without incident and it was immediately noticeable that the smaller ship, able to travel through the canal, was much less stable in the water than the large steamship, but otherwise equally comfortable in essence.

He had borne Adele's disappointment for a few days now; a slight chilling in her regard, as if he'd confirmed to her that she was right about him. It made him feel ungenerous, and he didn't like it. He'd never been ungenerous in his dealings with her, but then her requests had never had any kind of real impact on his life and schedule, signifying a delay to his plan.

He found her watching the sights of the canal pass before them—the foreign land that slowly and silently passed by, with its desert landscape and strange peoples.

"I suppose we could stop one day in Venice if you wish," he said as he reached her, taking her slightly by surprise.

She turned to him. "That would be wonderful. I have always wanted to see it."

"It is an interesting city, I suppose."

"Have you spent some time there?"

"Yes, in my youth, before..." He was going to say 'you,' but stopped himself. "We went—a group of us—over a summer. We traveled around Italy and France."

"I wasn't aware," she said, watching him.

"It was a long time ago." His mind traveled back to a wonderful summer he'd spent in Southern Europe with his circle of friends. It had been the best time of his life and he hadn't thought about it for a long time. All possibilities had been opened to him then and he'd been unaware of the realities of his future. "This time of year is not the best time to see Venice, of course."

"It doesn't matter," Adele said. The excitement in her voice was noticeable and he felt an irrational sense of pride having brought her pleasure and a slight flush to her face.

"We'll arrive in the morning; spend one night in Venice, then take the train the next day."

Adele's excitement was evident in her movements. She squeezed his arm slightly in gratitude—he expected it wasn't an action she'd been aware of.

It was a cold and rainy day when their ship sailed into port in Venice. He'd been right; it was a less than suitable day to go gallivanting around the city, but Adele didn't seem to be put off. She was dressed and ready when they sailed in, and they stood and watched over one of the railings, while the crew did their bit to prepare for arrival.

"It's beautiful," Adele said. Lysander didn't say anything. He wasn't exactly dreading the day, but neither was he relishing spending a rainy day sightseeing. Sighing, he decided he would see about getting them a pair of umbrellas. He'd sent directions to the staff to secure him two rooms at one of the finer hotels and they would see to the conveyance of their trunks and belongings.

Stepping onto the wet stone quay at Venice port, he turned to assist her off the gangway. As every port he'd seen—and he'd seen a few of late—Venice port was active and busy irrespective of the rain. They walked for a while before he found a general merchant's store, where he purchased two umbrellas that would functionally serve to protect them from the rain.

"Are you sure you want to spend the day here? We can go straight to the train."

"Of course I do. It is only a little rain. I wouldn't forgo seeing Venice for a little rain—a flood maybe, but nothing short of that."

"Then come this way," he said and urged her toward one of the smaller canals leading away from the port. A gondola waited for customers; its owner wrapped up in a heavy cloak. The man uncovered a bench at the center of the sleek, black vessel and Lysander held Adele's hand as she stepped onto its unstable floor. "Caffè Florian," he said to the man.

The boat moved smoothly through the quiet canals. It certainly wasn't busy on a day like this and the smell of the city was washed away and suppressed with the rain, leaving the whole city looking shiny and clean. Adele's eyes were large, taking in the sights of the ancient city. The only sounds were that of running water as it ran down spouts along the canal.

Lysander had never actually been outside in Venice during weather like this, having spent the rare rainy day inside during the summer he'd been here. The city appeared deserted, as if it was there for them to explore on their own. A few shops were open, lights shining out of glass windows, but only the rare person hurried along outside, seeking refuge from the rain.

The gondola took them down a maze of canals over the dark green waters until they reached the Piazza di San Marco. The square was also deserted and the only sounds were their own steps across the stones of the square. Adele stopped to survey its beauty.

"That is the Doge's Palace," she said, pointing at an ornate building occupying an entire side of the square.

"Yes, but let's bolster our resolve with some refreshments first." He urged her toward the cafe along another side of the square. "Then we can explore." She turned back to him, a broad infectious smile across her features. "Come. We will eat first."

They were shown to a table at the cafe he'd been to numerous times before. It was sparsely visited, compared to how it was in summer, when it was full of tourists, including, invariably, people he knew from London. Over the summer he'd spent there, it wasn't unusual to run into groups of people from his own wider circle of acquaintances as they visited the city.

He ordered pastries, ham, eggs and coffee—a hearty morning meal that would see them through the day. The rain persisted outside as they sat near the window. The dampness of the day made water condense on the windows inside the warm restaurant.

"Thank you for taking me here," she said again. "I do realize it is not a wonderful day for seeing Venice, but I will never forget that you gave me this opportunity." Taking in the décor of the café, her face was flushed from the chill outside and her lips were the color of a blooming rose. If he cared to admit it, she looked enchanting as she tore a piece of pastry, placing it in her mouth before bringing the small cup of coffee up to her mouth. "I don't normally drink coffee."

"It is what is done here." He took a sip of the thick, dark liquid, letting it coat his mouth and warm his tongue. The food was delicious, and when they'd finished, he could see Adele watch longingly out the window. "Well then, shall we proceed?"

"Yes," she said with obvious excitement. Opening the door, he led her outside into the atrocious weather. Their umbrellas were still waiting outside and the patter of the rain beat on them as they walked out from the covered walkway.

"Do you want to see the Doge's Palace?"

"I would love to."

Walking through the Palace's sumptuous halls for an hour, they would occasionally encounter another couple, but for the most part, they had it to themselves. Adele turned to see the pictures on the walls and the frescos on the ceiling— the treasures of the Church and another age. The rooms had a musty smell and after a while, he grew tired of the gold leaf and endless paintings—Adele drew his attention more as she tried to take in the overwhelming sights of the place. Reaching out, she touched a statue tentatively, feeling the texture of it.

"Come, let's walk outside for a while," he suggested. She turned to take his arm, joining him silently. For a second it seemed as though they belonged together. He was getting used to having her at his side.

Lysander breathed in the fresh air when they reached the outside. It was still raining and they reclaimed the umbrellas, before picking a street at random and heading down its narrow walkway, past shops and restaurants.

It felt as if they were the only two people in the world, and he was surprised at how comfortable he felt in her company for once—perhaps because her attention was completely absorbed by their surroundings. Her skirt was getting wet, but she didn't seem to notice. He wondered if he should cut this excursion short, but then felt he shouldn't be such a spoil-sport—neither of them were children and a bit of rain, for one day, would do no harm.

They walked down alleys, across squares and bridges. He'd lost track of where they were and they headed down narrow alleys that sometimes opened to small squares, some leading to dead ends at the edge of some canal. The architecture was varied and foreign—uniquely Venetian. They got lost in the maze of the city, before reaching the Grand Canal where they had to navigate down the canal to find the Rialto Bridge.

They weren't going anywhere in particular, just walking down random alleys to see where they went. It felt as though a private audience with a city put on display just for them.

Adele's eyes were caught by the jewelry in a shop window.

"Venice is known for its glass," he stated.

"My mother had a jewelry box that came from here. I don't know what happened to it; I think it went with the estate. I thought if I saw something similar, I would get it."

"Then let's look inside." He opened the door for her, fixed to buy her whatever she wanted. It would please him to, perhaps as an acknowledgment that they had a day where they functioned well together.

Her attention drew to a silver box with glass covering the top, a flower motif melted into it. He nodded to the clerk, who wrapped the box, before handing it over. Placing it in his pocket, Lysander paid for the trinket.

Adele had turned and was looking at some masks that were lining the wall of the shop. They almost seemed life-like as they stared out from the wall, some of them beautiful, some grotesque.

"It is forbidden to wear those, I believe," he said. Adele turned to him, her blue eyes seeking his. "Carnival masks."

"They still sell them."

"To tourists mostly. The craftsmanship is still appreciated, and if one must go to a masquerade, there is no alternative to a genuine Venetian mask."

"Do you have one?"

"Yes, somewhere." They stepped out into the rain again, the sound of it insulating them from the rest of the world.

"Could you imagine if they still had the carnival here?"

"It would be the biggest attraction in the world."

"I wonder why they stopped it," she said.

"It was almost a century ago. It was mandatory to wear the masks at one time; one could be arrested for refusing."

Curiosity and disbelief flittered through her features. "Truly?"

"A strange concept," he continued, "a time of year when one had to live without one's identity—in complete anonymity. Poor or rich, all were stripped of their identities—to exist without past or social structures for a time each year—without any consequences." He'd been told the history of the carnival in great detail when he'd been here before; it had appealed and fascinated him greatly at the time. He'd been young and had wished for it to still be done in these streets. "Nothing of what you were mattered when you walked the streets during carnival; you could be anyone, do anything—no matter how hedonistic." Adele's attention turned to him. "The structures of marriage didn't matter, nor the confines of position or office."

"Then how would one know who one dealt with?"

"One didn't. The purpose of the masks was to hide it all," he said. A slight frown flashed through Adele's features. "Any impulse could be acted upon, if you wanted. And people did, sometimes without discretion—which is why it was outlawed in the end."

"It seems like madness."

"Or liberating." That was how he'd seen it— complete liberation. But he'd been young then, looking for diversion and excitement.

She was watching him as they had stopped in the middle of the street, and she stood there holding her umbrella, looking at him intently. Her slightly parted lips and the breaths that fought the tight confines of her corset. He wondered what she would do if she was here during carnival, suspecting that her appetites were more daring that he'd ever expected of her. How far she would go—if she could be convinced to have intimate relations with a stranger in the streets of Venice?

Clearing his throat, he looked away—dismissing the picture his mind was trying to form for him. "How are your feet?" he asked.

"Truthfully, they are getting a bit sore."

"Then perhaps we should find our hotel." She nodded at his suggestion.

It took him a while to orientate himself, but once he did, he knew exactly where the hotel was. She walked ahead of him down the narrow alleys, and now, later in the day, the sights of Venice drew his attention less than the woman walking ahead of him—her straight spine, wisps of her hair escaping their confines and caressing the pale and thin column of her neck, the curve of her back and the swing of her wet skirt when she walked—the complicated woman in front of him—further complicated by the long and unpleasant history between them. Just the idea of her was loaded with resentment and grievances, but if they put that aside and he viewed her abstractly, she was quite lovely.

Turning to see that he was still behind her, she smiled, an impulse he'd seen her give to others, but never him. Watching her turn back, content that he was there, her wisps of hair floated on the air. He didn't even know how long her hair was, as he tried to imagine what she would look like with her hair down, flowing around her slim shoulders. It made him feel heated, but he was soon distracted by their arrival at their hotel.

They entered a sumptuously carpeted hotel and he announced them to a man waiting to attend, who preceded them toward a set of stairs leading up into the building. The hotel was decorated in the same style as the Doge's Palace, but the themes more related to the history of Venice and less biblical in nature. The hotel was a Palazzo that had been built during the middle ages, owned by a wealthy Italian family he'd met once.

Their trunks had been delivered and their rooms prepared, he was told. The man, in his black velvet jacket, ran through the notable people who would be dining at the hotel that evening, and Lysander recognized a few names. They were shown into two adjoining rooms, and after seeing to Adele, the man retreated with a sharp bow, closing the door behind him, leaving Lysander alone in the completely quiet room.

Walking to the window, Lysander looked down on the gray and rainy Grand Canal. The raindrops pitting the surface of the water across the stretch of the canal.

Pulling off his wet jacket and trousers, he hung them up on a clothes hanger on a hook in the wardrobe where his other clothes had already been hung. It was a few hours until they'd dine downstairs in the restaurant—hours to rest and recover. He was slightly chilled from the day spent in the rain, but not distressingly so.

Watching the rain streaking down the window pane, he lay down on the bed for a while, but he wasn't tired enough to sleep. He tried turning his thoughts to the days ahead, put they kept turning back to the day that was. It had been the strangest day he'd ever had, walking around Venice in pouring rain with a woman who had effectively enchanted him—one he couldn't touch. Lying on the bed, he listened to the rain and the ticking of a clock somewhere in the room. His thoughts turned again to his companion, who was safely consigned to her room, behind the wall in front of him. He wondered what she was doing.

Sighing, he put his arm back behind his head and considered her. She'd found pleasure walking around the streets of Venice; he'd indulged her and they had spent an unusual day together. He couldn't quite figure her out—too innocent for a villain, too guilty for an innocent. He didn't quite know what lay behind the cool, reserved exterior, but he did get glimpses of it.

He had wondered again what she would do if she was free from identity and consequences. There was no escaping the fact that those two things were of supreme importance, particularly in their dealings together. She was the faithless wife, the one who had embarrassed him, abused his trust, lied by omission—not to mention the impact on his life when he'd married her. He was probably going to have to divorce her; her notoriety in London amongst his peers left him with few options. It wasn't something he wanted to think about, but there were few solutions to the problems she had created.

But for a moment earlier that day, he'd wanted her. Heady desire had suffused him and it still warmed his blood now. He wasn't immune to the romance and the challenge of this city—the underlying hedonism that this city seemed to recall. He almost wished the carnival was still occurring, filling the city's streets with its possibilities, festivities and atmosphere of anything being possible, without consequence and underlying meaning—just the immediate and most superficial of desires. If it were, he could seek her out in this magical city and explore this unbidden attraction—without all the baggage and implications of their circumstances. She was, in essence, the one woman he couldn't have, and at the same time, the one he should be spending his desires with—if it hadn't been for all that had gone before.

But the madness of the city flowed in his blood, heating him. Sighing, he closed his fists, letting his fingers stroke the insides of his palms. He desperately wanted to touch.

His thoughts returned to the promise of the carnival, where he would seek her through the streets, find her. He imagined their ragged breaths as they found a quiet alley, where he could lift her skirts and she would reveal the deeper nature of her, their lovemaking echoing off the witnessing walls.

This mind's eye shifted, to her walking toward him, wanting him—offering herself. His hands ached to touch, hold the side of her hips as she rode him. Groaning, he placed his wrist over his eyes in an attempt to block the images out. He had the legal right to knock on the door that adjoined their rooms, but the moral obligation not to. Only the carnival would free him from those obligations and let him exorcise this desire that had been awakened in him.

Perhaps this city brought on a madness that filled his mind with thoughts he shouldn't have and his body with urges he mustn't have. It would pass. Tomorrow they would be on their way, traveling north, back to London.

Chapter 14

THE TRAIN LEFT VENICE STATION early the next morning. Adele had left Lysander to organize the details and the hotel had been helpful and efficient in moving their trunks to the train, and into their respective compartments. Adele felt her heart sink as the train moved away from the station; she was going home and she didn't really have any positive feelings about it.

It was still raining and the skies were gray, reflecting her mood perfectly. She was sorry to leave Venice; she'd only had a day to discover it, and it had been a day spent in the company of Lysander—which was unprecedented and not as difficult as she'd expected. It was a place that put ideas in one's head—a place of excitement and possibilities—a place to be explored with a husband; a true husband—a lover. There had been moments when the reality of their situation had slipped away, but it would always come crashing back—the disaster that was their marriage.

She was done thinking of the disappointment of her marriage; she'd spent years doing that and it had achieved her nothing but heartbreak. But equally, thinking of the future was just as fraught. There was only the present, as there had been yesterday, and today, Europe was passing in front of her—the repetitive clacking of the wheels, lulling her mind as it passed.

If she gave into her fears, the day would turn morose, which served no purpose; she was in Lysander's power—he would decide her fate. Once she knew, she could plan—try to salvage something of her life.

A knock on the door distracted her and an attendant stood on the other side. "Lord Warburton wishes to know if you will join him for tea," the smartly uniformed young man said.

"I will find him," Adele confirmed, closing the door with a nod to the young man. Turning back to her compartment, she wondered if there were any preparations she needed to do, but she couldn't think of them. She could have said no, but she felt that perhaps it was best to be agreeable to her husband during the time they were together. She didn't want any more strain between them than necessary; things were bad enough as it was. She would endure whatever was to come, and she would do it with grace.

Walking down the aisle of the train, she felt her way along the wooden paneling as the train lurched every once in a while. The dining car was lively, with a table at each window. Lysander sat by one of the tables, wearing a dark-gray suit of impeccable tailoring. He always dressed well— not perhaps in the latest trends, but with consistent and undeniable taste. He was looking out the window; she could see his eyes skip as the view rapidly moved along.

Greeting him, she sat down at his table. "It is a shame that the rain obscures the view," she said. He didn't respond, but turned to the waiter to request a cup for her. The waiter came and poured tea for her from the silver teapot.

"We'll be leaving Italy tomorrow, I believe," he said once the waiter had left. Somberly, Adele nodded. Each country they left seemed to take her further away from the life she'd run to and closer to the one she'd run from.

"Perhaps the weather will clear up as we head northward," she said with a thin smile. A plate of small sandwiches was placed in front of them, but Lysander didn't take any, instead returned his gaze to the window.

Adele hadn't known about his summer in Venice. It must have been before she'd met him. He'd been young then—arrogant and confident. Since then, he'd changed over the years; his youth had still clung to him when she'd first met him, but he'd developed into a man as time passed; the change obvious each time she'd seen him. The angry scowl never changed. It had been gone the previous day, but it was back now. The conversation equally strained.

"What were your plans in Australia?" he finally asked.

"Just to teach, I suppose. I hadn't thought much further." The silence stretched. His lips pursed and his eyes narrowed for a bit, then looked away. "Where else did you go when you traveled, the summer you went to Venice?"

"France and Austria, as well as Italy—Venice, Florence, Pompeii and Rome."

"It must have been an exciting summer," she said. She'd never been anywhere until Mr. Ellingwood took her halfway around the world, on the most exciting adventure of her life. This trip back to Europe, would by default, be the second most exciting. She couldn't even imagine spending a summer exploring Florence, Pompeii and Rome. She felt pure envy at the freedom he'd had in his youth compared to her.

"It was, I suppose."

"Will we be stopping anywhere else on the way?" she asked hopefully.

"No," he confirmed and Adele's hope sank. "You seem to be quite an enthusiastic traveler."

"I suppose I am. It is something I have learnt recently about myself."

"What else have you learnt?"

"That I am a half-decent teacher."

"Did you enjoy teaching?"

"I did. The children were wonderful." Adele's thoughts clouded over. It seemed their conversations tended to draw uncomfortable memories, no matter what they discussed. She had adored teaching children; having wanted her own for years now. She'd had mixed feelings on the topic when she'd been with Samson, as her children would be disadvantaged due to their situation, but she'd still been sad when her bleed came after Samson's death, finally closing the door on a child resulting from their lovemaking. That was another thing she had learnt about herself—her passionate nature and how she blossomed in the care of a tender man.

She noticed Lysander watching her, breaking through her musings. She tried to smile, but it came out too tight to be convincing.

"My aunt will be glad to see you," he finally said.

"It will be nice to see her," Adele said brightly, shifting her thoughts to a less confronting topic; although she wasn't sure how she would be received by Isobel. "Then again, she might not be so welcoming anymore."

"She blames everything squarely on me," Lysander said dryly. "She thinks I'm a right plod as a husband."

Adele smiled into her cup of tea. Isobel had never held back on her judgment of her nephew's behavior, even when Adele tried to make excuses for him. But her sympathy might have waned now, considering the actions Adele had taken.

"I am sorry my actions caused you embarrassment," she said. "In all that happened, I never purposefully tried to embarrass you. When… " she didn't say his name, because she knew Lysander tensed when she referred to him, "… died, I thought it would be best that I did so as well, releasing us both from this marriage. I thought it was the best thing."

The muscles in Lysander's cheek tensed and he looked away. He was so difficult to read sometimes. It was hard to judge what would offend him and what didn't. She couldn't always pick his reactions, and she had no idea how he would react to the present conversation. Even more confusingly, he seemed to not react at all.

"Perhaps you are not the best to judge such," he said sharply, after a while.

"How could it be anything but?" she asked, growing more heated, and Lysander gave her a warning look. She looked around to see if they were being observed. "For me, there wasn't a choice."

"Are you telling me you had no choice in abandoning your marriage and running off with a man not your husband?"

"It was no longer an option staying."

"Don't be so melodramatic. You make do. I made do."

"You abandoned our marriage the day after our wedding," she hissed. As she stared, she saw icy anger wash away the heated anger in him. "We never had a marriage. We had some pretense of a marriage; a terrible and cruel one."

His features softened a bit. "I did not purposefully try to be cruel. Admittedly, there were a few points when we were first married, when I was and I apologize for that. But on the whole, it was not my intent. You must understand that this marriage was not something I wanted."

"You made that abundantly clear."

"I suppose we both have things to apologize for."

"I thought if I died, you would be free to find a marriage you were more suited to," she said, pressing her napkin to her eyes to stop the tears that were pricking at their back.

"I acknowledge your intent—misguided as it was," he said stiffly.

On some level, Adele felt for the first time that she had a common understanding with him. It was a liberating feeling, releasing some of the tension, confusion and anger. It may not address the future and all its uncertainty; he'd said he didn't know what he was going to do, but she felt as if it did address the past and many of the grievances they had. Truly, she didn't want to fight with him, or be constantly at odds, tension gripping her every time he was near.

Leaning back, his gaze returned to the passing landscape. It even seemed brighter outside as the Italian countryside passed before them.

*

They passed into Switzerland and then into France, their slow progress back to London moving relentlessly on. Lysander dined each meal with Adele, and before long they were invited to dine with other travelers as well. Sometimes he wished travel wasn't such a social activity, but everyone sought amusement and diversion from the tedious hours with nothing to do but watch the landscape change—a diversion that finished when the sun went down.

Adele spoke competently of current topics, sometimes things she wouldn't have learnt at his country house at Devon. He came to realize that some of the things she knew where from keeping company with that man. Jealousy stole into him at those points—along with the knowledge that she would likely still be with him if he hadn't been unfortunate enough to succumb to a tropical disease.

She'd stated that she'd been happy with that man, and she never had been with him. It wasn't surprising; he'd never so much as tried to nurture their marriage, having been too distracted with how it came about and the things he'd lost because of it. Perhaps he had made a mistake all those years, ignoring her and refusing to develop any relationship between them. This was a new thought; he'd regretted the misery that his actions in this marriage had caused her, but he'd never considered the loss to himself.

As he sat watching Adele talking animatedly with a couple from Rochester, he wondered how this marriage could have turned out differently. It was his fault; he saw that now. He'd had no intentions of changing the nature of their relationship at the time she'd chosen to abandon him; he would have continued in exactly the same fashion. He'd even been angry at her death for changing the continuity of his current life, which waited for him back in London—Harry, Evie and Isobel, along with his clubs and his schedule—the life of an unencumbered bachelor, without the tedious designs of matrons on his bachelor status. But he wasn't a bachelor and he never had been. And now his life was confusing. He was dragging her back and there would be unpleasantness whatever he chose to do. He didn't want to be cruel to her; he had fully admitted that he had been at some points, where his anger had focused on her as the cause for all his misfortunes—while she'd never been the cause for their marriage. She'd had even less choice than him. Her resignation and acceptance of the union used to grate on him and he blamed her for her lack of objection to any of it—just accepting it in her steadfast and unassuming way. But then her subsequent actions had proven that she hadn't accepted it, but was opposed to his consistent rejection of their marriage, hers had expressed itself explosively with abandonment of station, marriage and propriety, all at once.

Chapter 15

ADELE SAT IN THE UPSTAIRS parlor of Lysander's London townhouse, a delicate teacup in her hand, resting on her lap. The house was quiet. They'd arrived last night and she stayed in the bedroom she'd only spent the night in a few times during her marriage. Lysander had gone out after having been remote and distant this morning as she joined him for the morning meal.

The oppression of the house was weighing down on her. It wasn't the house as such; it was their whole history. It was easy to forget when they were traveling and away from here, but now they were back. She drew a shuddering breath and let it go. She was back in London.

A knock attracted Lysander's butler to the outer door.

"Is she here?" Isobel's voice could be heard from downstairs. The butler directed her to the parlor and Adele heard the rustle of her dress as Isobel came up the stairs.

"Oh my dear, I cannot believe it. You are here. We were told you had died. It was so awful, but here you are."

Adele rose to embrace her friend, feeling relief that Isobel hadn't rejected her. She would understand completely if Isobel refused to see her ever again.

"It is so good to see you," Adele said, her eyes speaking more than she could manage to say in words.

Isobel sat down. "I have so wondered if I told you the wrong thing," she said. "I felt as though it was my fault."

"You only told me the truth and it was what I needed to hear."

Adele felt herself tear up and she fought them spilling. Isobel went to comfort her, but Adele turned her

119

attention to the tea service, not wanting comfort to make her feel even more distraught. Comfort was not what she needed right now; she needed distraction. "How are the boys?"

"They are well; getting older like all of us. Andrew thinks himself in love," Isobel said with an eye-roll.

"Does he? I would have thought he was much too young."

"Yes, well, you would think so, but he insists. He really is too young. She is a nice girl, but one doesn't quite know one's heart at seventeen." Isobel accepted a cup of tea. "I do hope he is treating you well." The conversation turned back to Lysander and Adele felt her teariness return. She refused to cry; she'd done too much of it and had sworn she was done.

"We are civil," Adele responded. "We've had a few spats, but on the whole, we are not ripping each other apart."

"Have you decided what you are to do?"

"Lysander hasn't informed me."

"He is a brute. I will have words with him."

"On the whole, he hasn't been entirely brutish," Adele said, and with the one exception she couldn't quite explain, he hadn't.

"Yes, he is, my dear. You have always been too forgiving of him." Isobel took a sip and placed the cup down. "Is he to petition for divorce?"

"I have asked, and he says not."

"He might simply be contrary. He is sometimes, when he doesn't get what he wants. I think he must, dear. You are more than welcome to stay with me when he does."

Adele looked over at her friend, amazed that she was taking this all in her stride. Adele knew that her actions would have caused gossip and conjecture that would have affected Isobel. "How did I get so lucky to get you as a friend?"

"Through the sheer bad luck of marrying my nephew."

Isobel said farewell shortly after, leaving Adele to her musings—particularly Isobel's belief that Lysander would have to divorce her. Her means and her status in society would be stripped back to nothing. Divorced women were hidden away in the remote countryside, ignored by even the local society. Isobel's offer to take her in would be generous.

The shunning by society wasn't, for her, the primary concern; she'd accepted that outcome when she'd left Lysander, but it was the loneliness she feared. She had suffered from it in Adelaide, even though her life had been her own. There were the other girls at the boarding house, but they weren't family.

She knew she couldn't go back to Adelaide. The fact that she had lied about being a widow and then been dragged away by her husband had ensured her acceptance back to Adelaide would be a long time coming. She had actually hated lying about her identity and wouldn't want to do it again. If she was to be divorced, she wouldn't have to—she would have freedom, but little to do with it.

*

Their days settled into a routine. They would dine together in the mornings, then spend the entire day apart. Adele would stay in the house and Lysander would spend every waking moment away from it. Isobel visited every other day, providing an hour of distraction to the long, tedious days. Each day, Adele expected Lysander to come and inform her of her fate, but the end of the day inevitably came and there was no change indicated.

In early evening, Adele searched through the books in Lysander's library, searching through the volumes that interested him. A few years ago, she would have gone

121

through this entire library to learn what topics drew his attention. There were more books on adventure and discovery, a few which must have been boyhood favorites. She ran her hand down the spines of the well-worn books from his childhood, trying to imagine what he would have been like.

A noise distracted her and she turned away. Lysander was coming down. She knew he was in the house, dressing for the evening. He'd hardly spoken to her since they'd got back. Book in hand, she moved to the stairway to started ascending, passing him in the process as he headed downstairs to leave the house. He nodded slightly as they passed.

"Lysander," she said, turning to him. He stopped his descent further down the curving staircase and turned back to her. He looked well in his dark formal evening wear and she wondered where he was going, but dismissed the thought—it didn't matter.

"Have you decided what is to be done?" she asked, needing an answer one way or another. He had said he wouldn't divorce her, but Isobel was sure that he would. "Am I to stay here in your house? Are you to send me back to Devon?"

Lysander looked uncomfortable. "As I have told you, I am unsure how to proceed." She suspected it was a substantial thing for him to admit uncertainty, going against his pride. "I am not being cruel by my lack of action. If I were to send you to Devon, I have no assurance you would stay there. Can you give me such assurance?"

Adele moved uncomfortably from one foot to the other. She wanted to give him assurance, but she also knew that life in the large empty house would be unbearable—soul-destroying.

Lysander saw her uncertainty and his features drew together into a frown. Turning to leave, he started descending the stairs again, but Adele wanted to stop him, to discuss this further. She still had no end to her situation.

"Lysander," she called again. He stopped at the base of the stairs, looking up at her.

Adele wrung her hands in front of her. She started talking, but it came out as a mumble.

"I cannot understand what you are saying."

Clearing her throat and shaking like a leaf, she tried to steady herself. "I cannot stand this emptiness," she said. "I understand that you will do what you must. I made choices and I am prepared to deal with the consequences. But I cannot be placed in a box and forgotten."

"What do you want me to do, Adele? If there is some way I can make this more bearable, I would," he said, losing a bit of the control he showed most of the time.

"I want..." she started. "Please give me a child."

Shock registered on his face, then his face darkened. He went to say something, but stopped.

"I need something to love," she said in a rush. "Whatever is to come, a child would make anything bearable."

The silence stretched on and Adele searched Lysander's eyes, but he turned abruptly and strode out the door. Adele didn't know if she had offended him, unsure she cared—they were beyond cordiality and needed to speak of basic needs at this point. It was a necessary topic. This might be the last chance she'd ever have of having a child, a family. From his perspective, it didn't matter if they divorced—a child was his. There was always the possibility that he would keep the child from her, but she didn't think he would be that cruel. She could raise the child, and he would have his heir—unless, of course, he wanted his children to be borne

123

by his future wife. The idea of a woman replacing her was strange, but she also wanted him to be happy. She wouldn't begrudge him happiness.

It didn't look as if he took the proposition well, but then again, he hadn't said no. At the very least, she'd made her desire known. It was now the one aim she had, but she needed him to give this to her.

Chapter 16

LYSANDER SOUGHT OUT HARRY in the reading room. He'd headed straight to the club after Adele's request, which had been so unexpected, he hadn't known how to react—sending his mind spinning and leaving him with an uncomfortable rush in his veins. He didn't know what to make of it; he couldn't quite grasp the implications. He needed to think.

Harry's displeasure at the news that, despite clerical errors, his wife was indeed still alive and currently residing in his house, had been obvious when they'd met a few days earlier. Lysander had entirely skipped the part about Adele knowingly letting the clerical error stand and absconding to Australia with the intent of deceiving everyone. It was an additional strike against her and Harry had quite enough as it was.

"And how is the strumpet today?" Harry asked over the top of his newspaper as Lysander sat down. Lysander bristled at the reference, even though he understood Harry's disregard and disrespect—driven by his judgment of her actions, but it wasn't an apt description. She was complicated, but she wasn't a common strumpet. "When shall you divorce her?" Harry asked.

Looking away, Lysander ran his nail down a seam in the armrest leather. The idea of divorce was whirling through his head, along with her proposition. An heir—it was an important issue.

Harry was watching him. "You must divorce her," he said and Lysander sighed. He knew Harry was set against her and would probably never change. Infidelity in women was unforgivable in his book, no matter what the preceding situation was. In all honesty, Harry wasn't the greatest enthusiast of the gender, with the exception of his own wife, whom he loved more than he'd ever admit, but he was still the only person Lysander could discuss his issues with.

"She has asked for a child," he said, straightening in his chair.

Harry folded his newspaper, placing it on the table and intertwined his hands together in his lap. Harry was silent for a moment, likely as shocked as he had been.

"I suppose the idea of an heir has some merit."

"I have waited longer than most."

"But is she the person you want to breed one on?"

"I certainly don't want to rush into another marriage."

Harry rubbed his chin and then sighed in a similar fashion as Lysander had a moment earlier. "If you had an heir, you wouldn't need to marry again."

"I would go as far as to say I lack certain talents in the wife management department."

"Yes, well, this time, she would be your choice."

Lysander wanted to shake Harry sometimes; tell him that there was nothing wrong with Adele, that it was just the situation that was bad. Not that it mattered; Harry wouldn't change his mind once it was made up. And he had determined to despise Adele.

Harry sighed again. "If you must breed an heir on her, you have to be seen with her. Otherwise, people will suspect that you are passing off one of the by-blows of that man."

Lysander took onboard what Harry was saying. It would be hard for him to present them as a reconciled party to all of London. It would damage his reputation further, but he had a duty to his name to produce an heir, and he also felt as if he had a duty to Adele to provide her with an outlet to her motherly instincts. Why must everything related to this whole situation be so difficult?

If he was honest with himself, and he succinctly refused to be, there was a certain excitement about the process involved. The need for an heir would supersede his obligations and he could lie with his wife. As much as he refused to admit it, he felt a heady excitement about the prospect. She was, in essence, the most forbidden woman. He almost wished this would have occurred to him back in Venice; it would have made a much less depriving few days. Venice had brought his youth back to him, and the freedom he'd felt then. His young self would have put all the consequences and implications aside, and would have succumbed to his wife's charms, probably have spent the two days in bed with his wife—likely wouldn't have let her see any of Venice at all.

Still, the idea felt dangerous. There was a certain danger to her. She had a gift for putting him in awkward positions, whether it be the public embarrassment she caused him or the highlighting of his own shortcomings. In the end, he always ended up feeling uncomfortable and disconcerted. He didn't know how exactly, but he would end up paying for this, if he did it.

"An heir now would give you complete control of your life. You could marry or not at your own leisure," Harry said. "I think the idea is growing on me.

Lysander had been afraid of that, because he'd hoped Harry would tell him a concrete reason not to do it—that the costs would be too high, but if he couldn't convince Harry, he would have trouble convincing himself.

*

Adele sat by the window watching the shifting weather outside. It was raining today, so she couldn't even spend time in the garden. She wished she was able to go for a walk, but Lysander hadn't been keen on the idea when she'd broached the subject one morning. His reticence was understandable, but equally, the benefit of having been hidden away in the country for years was that she had almost complete anonymity in London. She could walk around Hyde Park without stares and whispers. Although she knew that she wasn't inherently interesting; her actions had made her so, particularly if it became known that she'd tried to fake her own death. That would make her the gossip of the town. It was a topic Isobel had avoided.

If she was going to stay here, she needed to do something with her time, but this didn't feel like home; she felt like she was an unwelcome guest in Lysander's house. And for that reason, she couldn't settle, which unfortunately left her with little to do on a rainy day.

The familiar feeling returned—waiting for Lysander. She was waiting for him to return without having any idea when he would. She was waiting for him to answer. Waiting for him had been the norm, the central pivot of her life, the point her world was structured around.

*

Adele watched Isobel's children play at the table they'd set up under one of the old oak trees. The spring breeze rustled the leaves slightly, while the sun warmed them, making it a pleasant day to be outside. It wasn't summer yet, but they were having their Mayday celebration together this year. Adele had been looking forward to this day since she'd learnt they were coming.

"Is this some of Mrs. Hennings jam?" Isobel asked. "I don't know how she does it—the woman has a gift."

"Yes. She gave me a pot in the autumn. I have been saving it."

"It is just divine," Isobel said, scooping a portion with a teaspoon into her mouth and savoring the taste, her eyes closing with pleasure.

128

"You can have the pot," Adele said with a laugh, then she spotted Mrs. Smith, the housekeeper, moving speedily toward the house.

"Someone's coming," Adele said and watched Mrs. Smith hurry into the house to greet whoever it was. He's come, Adele thought. Putting down the plate she'd been holding, she ran back toward the house, feeling her heart beat with excitement. She'd suspected that he might come once he knew that Isobel and the children were joining them.

She ran through the house and out the front door, where she was met with the sight of Mr. Samuels, the rector who'd known the family as long as living memory, stepping down from his buggy.

Disappointment flared through her. She'd been sure this time. Trying to smile, she welcomed Mr. Samuels, but it came out more as a grimace. Mrs. Smith directed him to the festivities in the back and he eagerly followed through, thanking everyone for his invitation. Adele stared down at the long, empty driveway.

"He's not coming," she heard Isobel's voice behind her. "I'm sorry dear, but he's not coming. You must stop expecting him."

"How can I stop? He is my husband."

Isobel sighed. "He is not much of a husband, certainly not worthy the title."

Adele couldn't quite turn around; she didn't want Isobel to see how hurt she was. It wasn't as if she should be surprised—he never came, but she'd hoped she'd seen some thawing in his countenance toward her the last time they'd met.

"You must stop this," Isobel said. "You cannot continue expecting him. He will not come. You must stop pining for a man who doesn't even see you."

Adele's brow drew together in a deep frown. Tears stung the back of her eyes, making her vision blurry.

"You've spent years hoping he will love you back, but he never will. You need to make a life for yourself. He might be your husband, but in name only. He has always seen it that way, and he will not change. You're tearing yourself apart hoping he is something he is not."

Adele stared down at her shoes, nodding even though Isobel couldn't see it. She knew Isobel was right; she'd just had this ridiculous hope that things would change, that he would change, and she was making herself ridiculous and miserable.

"What do you do when you love someone and they won't love you back? I have tried to be perfect—everything I should have been, but nothing will please him." These things she'd never mentioned before were rolling off her tongue. "I have been the perfect wife. I have never stepped out of line. I have done everything I should have."

Isobel moved up to her side and put her arm around her shoulder.

"He does not see you."

The tears finally spilled. She was embarrassed about it, but she couldn't stop.

"You need to spend your love on someone who deserves it," Isobel said kindly, pity lacing her voice. "You have so much to give; you just need to find someone who sees and appreciates the amazing woman you are."

Adele tried to straighten her back, but struggled with the burden of this realization and the finality of it. She'd knew what Isobel said was true; she just hadn't been willing to accept it for so very long. She'd loved Lysander since the day they'd met and he had never seen her, seen any value in her, and the painful truth was that he wasn't going to change.

"You suffer and you suffer. There is no gold medal at the end of this—just a wasted life. Live your life, Adele. You owe it to yourself."

She nodded again, wiped her tears and tried to smile. There was a Mayday celebration to host and she never failed as a host. She was the perfect wife—attributes and values so ingrained in her, she wasn't sure how to be anything but. Letting go a shuddering breath, she tried to clear her morose mind so she could turn her attention back to the immediate needs. The thoughts about her life and what she needed to do with it would wait until everyone left her to the silence and solitude of this vast house.

Chapter 17

ANNOYED AND RESTLESS, Lysander sat in Evie's parlor. He didn't want to be there, but things would only get worse the longer he left it, and he'd left it long enough as it was. To mollify her displeasure at having been ignored, he'd had to buy her a trinket. But the truth was that he didn't want to be there. Evie was pacing, ranting at how embarrassed she felt at being completely overlooked.

It was her passion and liveliness that had drawn him in the beginning, but he'd grown tired of the dramatics, even before he'd left for India.

"You will, of course, be divorcing her," Evie said, her russet curls bouncing as she sharply turned. "Have you started proceedings? I was so happy for you when the news came that she'd died. And then for it not to be true. How fate is cruel."

"There had been a misunderstanding on behalf of the Colonial Office," he said, but he wasn't sure why he was justifying it. He didn't want to talk about Adele with Evie.

"You are a saint letting her stay in your house." Since he hadn't told Evie that was the case, it proved she knew more about his life and goings on than the things he told her. "You should free yourself of her at the earliest opportunity. You deserve so much better."

He knew full well that his wife's death had been seen as nothing but an opportunity to Evie, who fully intended to do everything in her power to take on the position herself. He didn't want to hear Evie's opinion of his wife. Neither she nor Harry had a true understanding of the relationship between them—not that he could claim to understand their relationship either.

"While she is here," he said. "It is only right that I not dishonor her."

"Dishonor her?" Evie stated, completely astounded. "She ran off with another man and you had to go retrieve her, and you are worried about dishonoring her? Lysander, darling, you are too soft-hearted and foolish for your own good. You cannot let yourself be deceived by her; she will say anything to have influence over you. Can't you see that?"

Taking a last sip of the drink Evie's housekeeper had given him, he bristled at the characterization of both himself and Adele. "Irrespective, I will not be delighting in your company while my wife is in situ."

Evie stopped her pacing and turned to him. "You cannot be serious."

"While my wife is in my house, I will not dishonor her," he repeated, standing and placing the drink he was holding on the side table.

"I might not be here when you decide otherwise," Evie said tartly.

"As you wish." But he knew it wouldn't be that simple. Evie saw a chance for marriage with his divorce and she wouldn't give up on that goal until the bitter end. "By your leave." Leaving, he felt relief as he exited her house. Sadly, Evie wasn't done—it would never be that easy, and she would play on his guilt and courtesy for everything she could. He would never marry her—not for the fact that she wasn't unsullied, because, unlike some, he truly didn't hold that against her. He just didn't like her enough to want to spend each day with her. But that wasn't an outcome that Evie would accept. Again he wondered why nothing was simple when it came to women?

His thoughts left Evie behind with notable speed, and he turned his attention to the troublesome woman in his house. What he'd said was right; he didn't feel right dishonoring her while she was here in London and he certainly wouldn't engage with other women while they were to conduct intimacy.

*

Lysander found Adele pacing around the garden. When they'd first arrived back in London, he'd forbidden her from leaving the house. In hindsight, it was perhaps a brutish request, but he just wasn't sure he could trust her to return.

Clearing his throat to catch her attention, he walked toward her. "You may go to Hyde Park if you wish," he said and she nodded her acknowledgment. Again he felt brutish, exercising his power over her. She didn't strictly have to comply, although compliance was expected in a wife, but he supposed he was testing her. "I have given your proposal due consideration," he said. Her eyes sought his, then she lowered them to the ground, placing a barrier between them. "As you know, an heir is a requirement for someone in my position, so it would represent an eventuality that would please us both." Her eyes came back to him and he saw hope and relief there, while noting his own reaction to having pleased her. Looking away, he cleared his throat again. "You will have to leave your door unlocked for me in the evenings."

"Yes," she said.

Feeling goosebumps, he reacted in a way he could neither describe nor justify. Suddenly, he felt distinctly uncomfortable. He was far from a prude, but this felt extremely awkward—perhaps because the purpose of this was conception and not pleasure. But that didn't change the fact that since their brief stay in Venice, he'd had forbidden thoughts about what it would be like laying with his wife. Unwanted thoughts returned to what he'd done when he'd first found her in Adelaide, but he dismissed the uncomfortable thoughts, ones that contravened the man he wanted to be—the man he thought he was. He did hope she had forgiven the trespass. "Unless it should prove too confronting for you."

"I am a grown woman; I think I shall manage."

The statement actually pleased him more than he'd expected, having worried that he'd deeply damaged her through his actions.

Exhaling, he left a weight lift off him. He'd dealt with the proposal and they'd agreed on a course of action. He'd probably left her a little too long without an answer—not on purpose; he just hadn't been ready to completely give himself over to the issue—including the fact that he would have to acknowledge his wife publicly in the process.

*

That evening, he didn't bother lighting more than one lamp, making his study darker than he usually kept it. Supper had been a silent and drawn-out affair, but it might have had more to do with his own tension than anything untoward with the actual meal. Adele had been flushed throughout—giving her a lovely countenance—which had actually made his tension worse.

Taking a deep swig of his drink, he wondered what she was doing—expecting that she would be anticipating him tonight. He was more nervous than he cared to admit and he tried to rid himself of it for fear that he may not be able to perform his duty. But the excitement and anticipation flowed in his blood no matter what he did, and he needed to take care in case he drank too much. Being unable to perform would be highly embarrassing.

Unbidden, the specter of Lieutenant Ellingwood moved around his consciousness like mist. As much as he tried not to think of it, Adele would compare him to her lover—someone she cared about, likely whose touch she craved. Not even his anger could compete with his nervousness tonight, but there was no use sitting there and deliberating. He wasn't one to shirk something due to discomfort.

*

The knock on her door sounded louder than it was in the quiet house. Trying the door, it gave readily in his hand and he paused for a moment, trying to gather his thoughts and get his breathing under tighter reign.

The room was dark, only a single candle lighting the space and he found Adele sitting at the head of the bed, her hair undone and flowing around her shoulders, covered by a white nightgown. He paused for a moment. She looked almost ephemeral like a wood sprite, sitting there with her legs tucked under her, her hands resting in her lap. Her eyes were large and bright as she saw him and he had an irrational urge to run over to her and kiss her, but instead turned to close the door silently behind him.

"Am I unwelcome?" he asked when he turned back to her.

Something crossed her brow for an instant, but he couldn't tell what it was. "No," she responded.

Feeling a moment of hesitation, he moved closer to the bed, praying to whatever god it was that saw to such things—that his member would remain hard this evening and not embarrass him—the member had been anticipating the evening since he'd returned to the house in the afternoon, but it hadn't become fully ready and he knew it wasn't right now either—the tension of the situation creating a dampening effect.

Not entirely sure how to proceed, he sat down on the bed after removing his vest. Adele moved herself along the bed to lie down, her knees tightly together and her ankles crossing as she did.

136

He'd never seen his wife naked, but then he'd never seen her in any state of undress, with the exception of their wedding night, which he didn't actually remember well due to the copious amounts of drink he'd had in his anger and frustration. The white nightgown showed her curves well. Her breasts were full and firm, and his body responded to the sight.

There would be no comfortable or fluid way of doing this and he just had to get on with it. Moving, he kneeled half way down the bed, unsure exactly how to proceed. Adele moved as well, positioning herself toward him, pulling her nightgown up her legs, automatically drawing his eyes to the revelation of skin along her thighs. For a moment, he was transfixed. As it turned out, there were no issues with his body achieving a proper state.

The noise of every moment sounded against the walls in the otherwise silent room as he freed himself and moved to the right position. Drawing a breath, he proceeded to push into her. Her body yielded slowly to him, allowing him into its delicious heat, divesting him of any other thoughts or concerns but the sensations that started flowing through him. Perhaps it was the length of time since he'd been with a woman or the provocative feeling that he was doing something forbidden, but he couldn't seem to muster his usual control. His body acted on its own, pushing into her with smooth, hard strokes, without him being able to exercise much control over himself. A shuddering release overtook him quickly and surprisingly, making him strive to force himself as deep into her as possible.

He didn't feel right laying down on her, even though he struggled to stay stable as the tension and resolution drained him. He felt disappointed. It had all happened so quickly; he felt that he hadn't even started accomplishing the things he wanted to—like a secret garden had been opened to him and he'd just rushed through it. But at least he hadn't embarrassed himself; he'd completed the task and had proven himself strong and resolute in the process.

Carefully, he withdrew from her, feeling sorry it was over so quickly. As he did, Adele pushed down her nightgown over her thighs—depriving him of any further look at her. He hadn't even laid a hand on her throughout the entire process. But he wasn't here to look or to explore; he'd completed his task and with a nod, he turned and quietly left.

Chapter 18

STILL UNDRESSED, ADELE SAT at her dressing table, brushing her hair with slow, fluid movements. The mild morning sun shone through the windows as she prayed for her own fertility. With excitement, she realized it could be that she was with child already. Their time together the previous evening had been uncomfortable and awkward, but there was still something in her that responded with pride. After all those years of being untouched and rejected, her husband had lain with her. It had been quick and to the point, but that was how her husband was in most things, she'd learnt. Again, she told herself not to read anything into it, just as she'd told herself the previous evening. It was a necessary interaction and she was grateful that he'd agreed to it. The temptation had been strong to delve into her long-standing and discarded infatuation for him—steeling herself for falling into the mindset that had caused her endless misery.

Giving herself over to her excitement, she looked toward her wardrobe. Not only was she potentially growing with child, but he'd also given her permission to venture out to Hyde Park, and she was going to take advantage of her new freedom this morning.

*

Sitting in the parlor upstairs, Adele heard as Lysander arrived in the afternoon. She hadn't quite achieved an understanding of his schedule and tensed as she heard him move up the stairs toward her. The door opened, and she put her embroidery aside.

"An invitation has arrived for a night of cards with Sir Allworth and his wife. I would like us both to attend," he said, staying at the doorway.

"Of course," Adele responded with a nod, not quite understanding the change in their circumstances. As for his actions, she'd assumed that he wouldn't take her anywhere, or introduce her as his wife—but if they went, he would have to. Again, she wondered at the change—whether it signified some real change in his attitude toward her.

The calm excitement at the future that had instilled in her that morning was now fading. She'd never traveled in his society and knew full well that she was a notorious woman. Nervousness gripped her insides, but she wasn't about to cry off. If he wanted her to present herself, she would—even for the purposes of ridicule and derision if she must. She had no illusions that she would be welcomed into his society with open arms.

"It is necessary," he said. "For the child's sake."

Adele hadn't even considered the implications for the child, but of course he was right. It was important that the child's paternity wasn't in question. A stab of disappointment flared through her as she realized his request had a completely practical purpose, having nothing to do with a change in consideration toward her. As he left, she chided herself on falling back to her old tendency of seeking his approval and admiration. He was never going to change and she would serve herself better to never forget that. Her attention should exclusively be on the wellbeing of this child—as his was.

*

Sitting in the carriage as it drove through Mayfair, in one of the more formal gowns the staff had retrieved from Devon, she tried to still her hands and hide the nervousness she felt. Her situation was her responsibility and she should be prepared to bear its consequences. Having chosen to run off with a man who wasn't her husband, she should be prepared to face the repercussions of her action, and now was the time to do so.

It was hard to make out Lysander's thoughts in the dark of the carriage, but he'd surveyed her gown and countenance as she'd descended the stairs earlier, and said nothing. As he hadn't look dismayed, she'd assumed that her efforts had been sufficient.

She steeled her resolve as the carriage door was opened by an attending footman on their arrival at their destination. Lysander stepped out, turning to help her out before leading her up to the entrance. Smiling timidly, she followed at his side, trying to hide the uncertainty she felt.

"Madame Allworth," he greeted the evening's hostess. "It is an honor to accept an invitation to your lovely home this evening. May I introduce my wife?"

"Ah, Lady Warburton," Mrs. Allworth said. "The elusive wife. We've always known you had one, but had always wondered what manner of sprite you hid away in the country. And here she is—a lovely creature." The woman smiled, but there was a certain tightness to it as her traveling gaze held a hard edge. At least politeness kept their opinions at bay, Adele thought.

Lysander turned slightly. "Harry, you remember Adele."

"Of course I do," Harry said, not quite looking her in the eye. She'd met him a few times and she'd never liked him; he'd called her frail as a bird the first time she'd met him and she hadn't quite warmed to him since—not that there was much to warm to; he'd dismissed her as readily as her own husband had.

As they walked into the salon, Adele prayed that Lysander wouldn't leave her on her own. There wasn't a single person in this room that liked her and that included the two men standing next to her. She smiled bitterly at the thought.

"Would you like a refreshment?" Lysander asked. She nodded, but regretted it as he moved away to the table serving refreshments, leaving her in the company of Harry.

"How is it being back in London?" he asked without much intonation in his voice.

"Hyde Park is a gem," she said with a smile, while noting the whispers and attention she received from the other attendants.

"Bit of a walker, are you?"

"Yes, I suppose." And with that, they had nothing further to say until Lysander returned to the relief of both.

*

"I think the evening went well," Lysander said as they traveled home again.

"Yes," she agreed, thinking back on the uncomfortable evening she'd suffered through. People's curiosity about her was consistent, even though they did try to hide it. Not being much of a card player, she'd stood by when Lysander had accepted the obligatory game—it had after all been the purpose of the evening. They were the first to leave, but it was already late. Society in London tended to run on a later schedule than elsewhere.

Leaning her head back, Adele congratulated herself on surviving her first foray into society. And without incident, too. She didn't deceive herself into believing she was accepted, but neither had she been cut.

The carriage ride wasn't long and Lysander took her hand when he helped her out. She felt the contact much more than the mere touch justified and wondered if he'd come to her that evening—not feeling comfortable asking.

142

She would prepare in case he did, telling herself sternly not to let her mind attach undue meaning to these intimacies. After returning to her room and undressing, she combed her hair, trying not to feel the anticipation running through her body. The previous night hadn't, by all accounts, been a riveting encounter on its own merits, but their history made it important beyond the mere mechanics of it.

Stopping the slow strokes of her hair, she listened to the movement in the house. Lysander was coming up the stairs and she waited to hear what he did. A slight knock on her door made her breath hitch.

"Am I unwelcome?" he asked when he moved inside the door, in exactly the same way as the previous evening.

Placing her brush down, she turned toward him. "No."

He nodded slightly and looked around the room as the moment of awkwardness stretched. Adele moved to the bed and placed herself on the covers, tension making her body feel heavy and stiff. She couldn't help herself watching as he took his jacket off and continued to undress, his movements slow and meticulous. She was nervous again, anticipating what was to come—and with a more pronounced hint of curiosity along with dread and resignation.

He left his shirt on and she would see that he wasn't entirely unprepared for the activity to come. As he kneeled on the bed in front of her, she felt heavy anticipation as she spread her thighs for him. Unlike the previous night, he didn't position himself immediately; instead letting his eyes linger on her for a moment. Adele felt a spear of concern that he'd changed his mind and regretted his decision to seek her out that night.

"Did I hurt you?" he asked. *More than you'll ever understand*, she wanted to say, but knew he was referring to the previous night. "If this will be uncomfortable for you, we can forego and recommence another night."

"No, I am fine. I wish to proceed."

With a nod, finally, he moved, shifting to position himself between her thighs. His entrance smoother this evening; her body seemingly a little more willing to accommodate him, and she felt herself stretch as she yielded to him, taking him with some effort. Biting her lip, she tried to sort the things that were going through her mind, and the mismatched signals from her body, purposefully quelling any sensations that were unnecessary.

Withdrawing, he pushed into her again and she felt the jolt of sensation as he buried himself deep inside her. She'd discovered the pleasure of a man's bed, but in another man's bed. She couldn't afford to pursue that here, with him, because there were such complexities between them. Lysander was going to divorce her and she couldn't afford to spend another ten years pining after him, dreaming of just this. She closed her eyes.

His movements grew firmer and she felt the pleasure of it caress her insides, refusing to feed its gentle insistence. His body drew nearer; until now he'd kept his distance as much as practical. His hand moved to her hip, urging her hips closer to his. His groan of pleasure drew one of dismay from her; she wanted to just give herself over to this primal, base undertaking. Keeping her eyes firmly shut, she tried to distract her mind.

Then she felt his lips on hers, the merest touch as first, growing firm. The touch unlocked something in her, which she unwillingly lost control over. He deepened the kiss and it broke through every barrier she'd ever managed to place. Her body flared with fire; sensation stealing through every part of her. Her whole body tensed around him, urging him deeper with desperate need. Their tongue met in exploration and her body suffered shocks of deep, piercing pleasure as his thrusts came to full emersion.

She needed more, much more; her hands ripping at the buttons of his shirt, giving way by force to reveal more of him, his chest and skin. Warm, hard muscle met her hands as she let them roam over his chest and along his back. He slowed, and again Adele felt a spear of concern that things had gone too far for him, that he was unwilling to be touched by her. Seeking out his eyes, she couldn't make out any meaning in them. He was staring down at her in stillness. Her core still pulsed around him in belated response.

Slowly, he leant down and kissed her—his lips soft and parted. The pleasure of the kiss suffused her mind and push away the confused apprehension she felt. She felt the tip of his tongue run along the sensitive inside of her lips. Mentally, she begged him not to stop; her body was wracked with painful tension, and he seemed to hear her beseechment, because his hips ground into hers, sending sharp waves of pleasure through her. His hands traveled along her backside, holding her to him, increasing the urgent friction between them.

Her body moved in unison with his, meeting each thrust, drawing as much sensation out, as small moans escaped when it became too much and she started to violently convulse around him. He slowed for a while as her body completed a series of writhing convulsions, then he kissed her again, leaving her no room for air or peace. His tongue demanded entrance and explored her mouth, before moving to her neck, teasing her skin as the hardness of him inside her slowly ground into her. Her release hadn't even addressed the painful tension she felt.

His hands urged her arms up above her head, where his other hand gently held her wrists as his fingers ran along the sensitive skin of her underarm, eliciting small moans from her as he teased her with gentle but ardent undulations from his hips. She could barely breathe, feeling completely undone both physically and mentally. This was everything she'd ever wanted—being desired by her husband, having her body worshiped by him.

More forcefully, he moved into her, drawing out the friction between them, sending new and powerful sensations cascading through her. She was completely at the mercy of this, every bit of her body in tune with his movements and ministrations. Her breath searched uncontrollably for air and his warm hand still holding hers above her head as his movement became more forceful, driving into her, to a new, shattering release. Arching into his release, his groans filling her ears and her mind as shudders wracked him. Welcoming him, she opened her body to his as much as she could.

His weight descended completely onto her when her mind gained some semblance of order. Her limbs tangled in his and she felt like crying, but also too uncertain to move. Withdrawing from her, he pushed himself back to sit on the edge of the bed, looking confused and maybe even dismayed.

Adele turned on her side, away from him. She couldn't quite get a handle on her own emotions as all her feelings seemed to have rushed back, leaving all her work to get rid of them for nought. He shouldn't have kissed her; it was the kiss that had done it—undone her. She refused to turn and acknowledge him as he rose and left.

Chapter 19

AFTER A FITFUL SLEEP, ADELE woke. The thoughts of the previous night returned to her immediately as she lay in bed. The kiss—it haunted her. Why had he done it? It wasn't his right to take it. Actually, the whole idea around what his rights just hurt her head to think about. It seemed ridiculous to say that a man wasn't allowed to kiss his wife, but under the circumstances, due to their distance and separation, he shouldn't have done it.

He'd unlocked the want she'd carried for him for so long, even as she'd thought she'd managed to get rid of it, but it had flared to life and he had given of himself. Her fingers still tingled with the touch. Closing her fist, she tried to make the lingering sensations go away, but they refused to budge, along with all the after-effects on all her other senses—taste, touch, smell and sound. He'd intruded on all of them.

She decided that she needed to go for a brisk walk. The coolness of the spring morning would wipe away these ghosts. After having Kathleen help her dress, she left the house, with her bonnet firmly in place and a parasol in case it rained, or the sun shone, or some ruffian became rude. She just felt as though she needed something in her hand.

*

Walking much further than she'd intended, she marched across the vast green space, almost catching her skirt between her legs a few times in her relentless pace. It was too early for most, certainly for people there with the aim of being seen. Finally, she sat down on a bench to let her heart slow. The bench was covered with dew, but she didn't care.

The images and sensations she'd run from returned immediately and she groaned with dismay. She knew it; she'd fallen right back into the trap that had held her for so long. She had to be harder than this. He was going to divorce her and she should be looking forward to the freedom and the idea that she wasn't beholden to anyone—someone who took with no thought to the consequences.

Adele had walked so far, she was absolutely exhausted when she returned, and famished. Ordering her breakfast brought to her room, she needed the comfort of her inner sanctum. As the house was quiet, she assumed that Lysander had gone out to do whatever it was he did during the days.

"The Master has left a note for you," Lysander's manservant said as she moved toward the stairs. "I asked Kathleen to place it on your dresser."

"Oh, thank you," Adele said, turning up the stairs. She had no idea what this note would say. Perhaps he would apologize for the previous evening—for engaging her emotions and desires when he shouldn't have. But it wouldn't; he'd have no idea what he'd done or what it had cost her.

Please accompany me to the opera this evening if you should be so of mind.

Your Servant, Lysander

Adele read the note over and over, like she used to do to dissect every possible intention he could have put in there. He was asking and not demanding, which was a change. Perhaps the previous night had highlighted the need for reason in him as well. Turning the note over to see if anything was written on the backside, she noted her name was written on one side of the folded note, written in his beautiful script with a large flowing 'A.' She scrunched the note up and placed it back on the table. The opera. She'd never been to the opera—a place that required a husband's accompaniment. There was something very attractive about the idea that her husband was taking her somewhere only he could, as though she was achieving a status that had previously been denied her. But she couldn't think that way—he was letting himself be seen in public with her for the sake of their child. Her hand traveled to her stomach; its flatness taunting her hope.

She couldn't deny that she was curious about the opera. It was both mature and a little bit risqué. She did want to experience it, and she should be grateful as her future as a divorced woman lay in a small cottage somewhere unseen.

*

When Lysander returned a few hours later. Adele had taken to her room, he was informed. Striding upstairs, he gently knocked on the door. The idea of attending the opera had come to him in the morning. He wasn't normally a fan of the over-dramatic, but it had suited his mood that morning.

"And have you decided to accompany me this evening?" he asked, almost a little teasingly. He knew she craved new experiences and this would please her.

"I am afraid I do not really have anything appropriate in my wardrobe," she replied, looking sorry and disappointed. At some point, he'd grown to despise that look, having had it directed at him a few times during their travels. "My wardrobe is mostly suited for church fetes."

"Ah," he said. "Although I do suppose it is not an insurmountable barrier. We could potentially find something among the more ready-to-wear stores. Perhaps not the most distinguished of dresses, but I am sure we can find something that will do for the evening. Tomorrow you can call the dressmaker and have a proper one ordered."

"I'm not sure…" she started, but stopped and shook her head slightly. "I don't know how long it will take to find a dress."

"Surely it shouldn't prove that hard. Come," he said holding out his arm. He hadn't intended on taking her shopping that day, but when the idea presented itself, it didn't seem like a distasteful one. Spending the day with her reminded him of Venice. He ordered the carriage to be brought out for them and they waited a few moments in the vestibule in silence. Adele looked flushed and lovely. Her walk had made her cheeks rosy, and her lips full—perhaps that wasn't the walk. Her trim waist, and her hips were buried under yards of silk. He felt a strong urge to drag her upstairs, back to bed, where he'd discovered her nature the previous night. He exhaled slowly, letting his breath expel some of the thoughts that were nipping at his mind.

He'd been angry this morning, furious in fact—the ghost of Samson Ellingwood had taunted him again, having coaxed the passion in her. He'd spent months on end ensconced in her bed and in her body, and he, her husband, was only there on reprieve for the sake of filling her belly with child. They were childish thoughts, he knew, but he couldn't help feeling them. He knew at the core, it was his fault, but he still didn't have to like it, any of it. But it was all too late now, the die had been cast and the consequences were clear. The time for choices was past.

Moving to the door, he heard the carriage pulling in. "Come," he said as he walked outside and ordered the carriage toward Regent Street.

"It's been a while since I've been to Regent Street," she said once the carriage was in motion. "I used to go quite a bit when I was younger, perusing the store fronts."

"Admittedly, I go very rarely."

"I suppose it is not a favorite activity of yours?"

"Decidedly."

"I can do this on my own," she said and his eyes left the scenery passing by to find hers. She seemed to be considering him.

"I am sure I can manage for a day. No doubt it will be unbearable, but I will muster through." He was jesting and she seemed to take it as such. He watched as she turned her gaze away.

It didn't take them long to arrive along Regent street, which was busy with shoppers. There were women of every age, and men of a certain age—the young ones who seemed to spend an inordinate amount of their concern on their appearance.

They found a store that offered ready-to-wear dresses. The store itself was warm and sumptuous in the way the French preferred. There was finery of all sorts and he felt as if he was intruding on a boudoir, a forbidden place filled with lace and silks, dripping in womanliness.

Adele spoke to the proprietress, an older French woman who would have been a great beauty in her day. The woman seemed to know exactly which dresses would suit the occasion and urged Adele to follow her along to the display of dresses. Lysander sat down on the red velvet sofa next to the dressing pedestal and the large gilt mirror.

Adele walked back toward him. "She says the fashion runs to dark, heavy fabrics."

"I doubt anyone would know the fashion better than she."

"She is getting a dress," Adele said, looking slightly uncomfortable. The woman returned with a dark bundle on her arm and waved Adele over to the curtained dressing area, where she disappeared into the hidden places only women went. Lysander looked around the store and out to the street. This dress would be dear, but he didn't begrudge her—feeling slightly ashamed that his wife didn't have the appropriate dress for such entertainment.

He wondered what entertainment Lieutenant Ellingwood took her to and if he provided her with the dresses she needed. Perhaps they spent all of their time in bed. A mere lieutenant wouldn't have the means to provide her with the entertainment and wardrobe that he could, unable to help competing with this man, for which he had the compelling and unfair advantage of still being alive.

The heavy curtain drew aside and Adele emerged, wearing a dress made of dark velvet. Her skin looked creamy pale in contrast and his breath drew as she emerged. She looked lovely as she took her place on the pedestal and women surrounded her, adjusting the dress to suit. The dress had short sleeves and her bare arms rested at her sides as she let the women do their work. The intention of the dress was that she wear long gloves with it, covering up her arms.

"It pleases, yes?" the proprietress asked him. She was justifiably smug in her presentation and creation. He nodded slowly, not distracting himself for long from his wife's form, feeling himself tightening. It was just a dress, but the effect of it was stunning—the dark color which contravened the prevailing brighter daytime colors in mode at the moment. The neckline at her back was lower, subtlety revealing pale skin on which a wisp of escaped hair lay, teasing.

"It will do," he said. "Will it be ready for this evening?" The woman made a wincing noise, which he knew was part of the negotiation process. Adele was measured, pinned and outlined while he finished the negotiation for the dress, for which the French woman drove a hard bargain, because they both knew he wasn't leaving without purchasing the dress.

He waited while Adele was taken to the back of the store to dress again, watching out the window where the weather was darkening.

"I wasn't aware a ready-to-wear dress would be of such quality, but it is a lovely dress. Thank you," she said and he turned to her.

"You are welcome."

"The dress needs some gloves," she said and moved toward a display.

"Yes," he agreed following her to stand by her, to survey the selection. She picked up a set of long, dark silk gloves.

"Do you think anyone will notice that these are not an exact match? A lighter green would also go well."

"Or these," he said picking up the gloves that were a similar color to her skin.

"You think these are better?"

"They are tempting."

"Tempting?"

"The color of skin, but not skin. A representation of the skin underneath, of the hidden—showing what is there, but impossible to touch." His thumb stroked along the silk of the gloves in his hand. "A bit of cruelty."

"We are not cruel," she said and reached for the gloves with her already gloved hand hiding her skin away, forbidding accidental touch.

"Aren't you?" He didn't relent his grip on the gloves as she made to take them. Her eyes sought his as they stood impossibly close in an innocent exchange. The amusement of their exchange shifted to something else, something more grave. "I never meant to be cruel," he said quietly. Her eyes moved away from him and he yanked slightly on the gloves so they snapped back to him. "I do know that much of the responsibility lies with me." His eyes moved lower. He wanted to kiss her and she was close enough that he could just reach down. It might not be entirely appropriate, but she was his wife—except she was the wife he was divorcing, which meant he really, really shouldn't.

She broke away first, clearing her throat. "I appreciate you saying that," she said, turning her attention back to the table. "I think I perhaps need some binoculars as well. I understand they are an encouraged accessory."

Lysander felt the loss of the moment, as it slipped away and the reality of the place and circumstance returned. "Of course," he said, looking around to see if the appropriate accessories were available here or whether they had to go elsewhere.

Chapter 20

THE DRESS ARRIVED AFTER supper. Adele had worried all afternoon that it wouldn't be ready in time, but there it was and it arrived in a large paper box which the maid had carried up to her room.

Adele was both nervous and excited for the evening. She also felt light because Lysander had essentially apologized to her and she had accepted his apology, believing him when he said he hadn't intended on being cruel.

The maid laid the dress out, then came and assisted Adele with her hair. Once on, the heavy fabric of the dress kept her firmly encased, the material feeling lush and rich under her hands. She looked beautiful, the darkness of the dress making her skin glow. She donned the long gloves and Kathleen helped with the little buttons at the wrists.

Taking one last look in the mirror, Adele left her room, wondering if Lysander would be moved by her gloves, which he said teased and forbade. As much as she urged herself not to, she wanted him to be moved by her, for a dull ache for him had settled deep in her belly and she couldn't shake it now. She hoped he would come to her tonight.

"The dress suits you," he said as she entered the parlor. She saw appreciation in his eyes and she flushed slightly, feeling breathless in the tight bodice. "Are you ready to leave?"

Adele nodded and followed him as he walked to the door. He looked handsome in his formal evening wear, reminding her of the young man she'd met so many years ago—arrogant and confident, assured of his place in the world. He still was, she supposed; hers was a little less so, but she was content for the moment. She checked herself as he helped her into the carriage—she shouldn't get used to this; it had a specific purpose and it wasn't to pretend to be like this, because they weren't merely a husband and wife out for an evening's entertainment.

The carriage was dark inside, with the only light intruding from outside as they passed.

"Will Harry be there tonight?" she asked. She hoped not. Harry made her withdrawn and uncomfortable. Beneath his politeness, there was no doubt what he thought of her.

"No, he has other plans." Adele hid her sigh of relief and then pressed her hands together to hide her nervousness, which only escalated as they drew near.

The theater was brightly lit, with handsome couples walking into the building—and she was about to be one of them. The reception hall was covered in rich carpet, gold candelabras and murals on the walls depicting dramatic scenes from well-known plays. The ceiling was high, like a church and there was a pervasive hum of conversation. She had never seen so many finely-dressed people in one place and had to stop herself from gawking as Lysander moved her into the space.

She stepped closer to him as he stopped and greeted someone, suddenly feeling shy. These people would all know what she did and she knew Lysander was being judged on her actions. Suddenly she felt the weight of the embarrassment and ridicule he'd felt, and appreciated that he would suffer this for the sake of the child they were hoping for.

The man was saying something about a property he'd purchased, his great big whiskers of his sideburns twitched as he spoke. His wife was elderly, covered in a brown silk dress that was ill-fitting. She seemed kind though as she smiled at Adele.

"Are you looking forward to the evening?"

"I am," Adele responded. "It is my first opera."

"Oh."

"I usually prefer the country." That wasn't strictly true, but she didn't want to cause Lysander embarrassment by calling their history and relationship into question.

"Understandable," the woman said. "But the delights of the city do call on occasion. I hope you find the evening enjoyable."

"I am sure I will." As far as conversations went, that had gone well enough. Whatever the woman thought of her, she hid it well; although she looked kind enough to perhaps overlook indiscretions. Adele liked to think so anyway.

They were moving on, amongst the crowd of people. There had never been so much finery and jewels in one room, she thought.

"Are you fine?" Lysander asked.

Adele let go of her tight grip on his arm. "Of course, I'm sorry. It is very crowded. I am not used to such crowds."

"It always is. For most, it is the true purpose of these evenings—to greet and be seen."

"Do you know most of the people here?"

"Yes."

"I only know you, I think."

He was going to say something, but another man's presence interrupted him and he was drawn into conversation. Adele surveyed the room, watching the women and the men, all dressed to impress each other. In this dress, she didn't feel out of place, but she felt she was well up to standard. And then they moved again.

"Lysander," another man said. "Excellent evening. You know my wife, of course. Of course you do; you've known each other for years, haven't you?" Adele's attention was drawn to the couple, particularly the woman who seemed to have known Lysander a long time. She bore the confidence of someone who had always belonged in this society and who had never had occasion to question her station.

"Alterstrong, you look well," Lysander said.

"And who is this?" the woman asked, turning her attention to Adele, her voice strong and crisp like a bell. This woman was beautiful. She had golden hair and blue eyes, all complemented by a dark orange dress; its material catching every light in the room. "Is this your wife?" The woman's attention turned questioningly back to Lysander. "My word, I never thought we'd see the day. I am pleased to make your acquaintance. My name is Cassandra."

"Adele," she responded, nodding slightly. The woman's renewed survey made Adele feel uncertain. "Lys had always told us you existed, but we had started to disbelieve him, but here you are. And such a pretty face." Cassandra threw another look at Lysander before returning her attention to Adele. "That dress is stunning, my dear."

Adele flushed slightly at the compliment and Cassandra's attention returned to Lysander, and started talking about some event they'd held. She was animated and absolutely charming. She called Lysander 'Lys,' Adele noted. The tension in Lysander drew Adele's gaze to him. He watched the woman's hands and when Cassandra placed her hand on his arm in a familiar fashion, he held his breath.

Frowning, Adele watched his reactions to this woman and then suppressed a gasp as she wondered if he'd had an affair with her. She watched them for a bit longer, watched as this woman turned her attention back to her husband. No, it didn't fit. This woman was teasing Lysander.

"It was good to see you, Lys, wasn't it darling?" she said to her husband, who mumbled agreement, which Adele guessed he always did to his wife's suggestions. "Perhaps it might not be a bad idea to have you over for dinner sometime, especially now that your wife has turned out to be more than a phantom."

Adele smiled at the comment, not really knowing what else to do. Lysander nodded awkwardly. "Of course," he said. Perhaps Lysander agreed with everything she said as well. Her manner seemed to indicate that she expected her demands to be followed.

The bell rang and everyone's attention simultaneously turned to the stairs. Obviously, they were being asked to take their places in the theater itself. Adele didn't feel like moving; there was something preying on her mind, demanding attention. She couldn't quite identify it, but it sat in the back of her mind burning—something important.

"Come," he said and held out his arm for her, and they moved toward the stairs. When they started moving up, Lysander's eyes moved to Cassandra's form as she ahead of them.

It struck her with certainty and finality. It was the only thing that fit. "You're in love with her," she said quietly.

He ignored her or didn't hear her, so Adele repeated her understanding again.

"Don't be ridiculous."

She stopped moving, her mind on fire with the implications of what she'd learnt. Thoughts were rushing around, competing for her attention. She tried to search for answers in his eyes. They were holding up the migration upstairs and Lysander urged her to move.

"Please don't lie to me," she said to him.

He looked around feeling uncomfortable. "It was a long time ago. Now come. This is an awkward place to stop." She let him gently pull her forward and down the hall toward their booth, which was dark when they walked through the heavy curtains, coming out to a place with two gilt chairs and a view over the loud and vast theater. Taking her seat, Adele watched as Lysander sat down next to her, a tight expression on his face.

"Are you in love with her?"

"Of course not."

"Were you in love with her when we married?" Adele asked, watching him intently.

"Adele, please," he said in low tones. He wasn't looking at her.

Adele gripped her hands tightly in her lap. He had been in love with another woman when he'd married her. So much of their history made sense now—his anger and rejection. It dawned on her that she'd never stood a chance at his affections. He must have hated her. Both of their lives had been wasted by this marriage and throughout he'd pined for another woman.

The burning shock inside her gave way to sheer desolation. She'd caused him endless degrees of suffering and she'd had absolutely no idea. She had dashed his hopes and dreams, leaving him with a burden he couldn't abide looking at.

The lights were being extinguished and the stage was prepared. Adele pulled out the little binoculars she'd bought for the occasion and once the singing started, she brought them up to her face to cover the tears that had started flowing. She tried her best to remain silent.

The truth was bitter, but it answered all the questions she'd had. It also confirmed that there had never been any hope.

"Do you wish to leave?" Lysander asked quietly after a while and Adele nodded. She didn't want to be there. She wiped her tears with her gloved hands, feeling the stains soak into her fingertips and tried to smile. "Come," he said and rose.

Chapter 21

ADELE WOKE UP TO A DARK and cloudy day, which seemed to suit her mood. She wasn't entirely sure what it was about the previous night that had shaken her so much, but it had. As much as she'd tried to convince herself that she was over her misguided loyalty to Lysander, the idea that he had been unavailable and suffering in their marriage had hurt tremendously. It felt as if something had died—finally broken irreparably.

But she couldn't quite shake the melancholy of its aftermath; it clung cloyingly to her and everything around her. She would recover from this, she knew—she hoped. She wasn't entirely able to see her future at this point, but she knew she would be fine—she just needed to recover from this. He had been right to hide this from her. If she had found out a year ago when they'd still had a live marriage, at least in her mind, she would have been absolutely devastated. It was hard enough to deal with it now that their marriage was effectively over.

Adele's thoughts returned to the woman she'd met last night—Cassandra—the woman Lysander had been in love with, and to whose presence he to some degree still reacted. She could see what would have attracted him; the woman was so entirely assured of herself and her position—two things Adele had never been. She'd never truly belonged to the society of her husband and he'd hidden her away. She'd always thought her origin in trade had driven his actions, but the answer was actually worse.

Cassandra was married and Adele tried to turn the situation over in her head, to find a way for Lysander to be with her, but the truth was that he'd lost the chance—she was married, and seemingly, happily so. Adele felt pangs of discomfort and guilt as she thought of it. As she knew from experience, living as man and mistress had some severe drawbacks, but a man and woman who belonged together sometimes needed to be with each other, marriage convention or not. It did hurt her to think that the Alterstrong marriage would have to disintegrate for Lysander to be happy, likely causing the misery of Lord Alterstrong in the process. Why couldn't people just be happy? Why must someone always get hurt when love was involved?

A knock on the door disturbed her. "Adele, are you there?" she heard Isobel's voice. Adele tried to smile as Isobel entered the room. "What's the matter?" Isobel rushed over to the chair beside her, taking her hand with a look of grave concern in her eyes.

"Nothing," Adele said with a quick smile she didn't have the energy to maintain. "How are your children?"

Isobel was watching her intently, unconvinced by the change in subject. "You look unwell."

"I just had trouble sleeping last night. I am a bit tired." It certainly was true; she hadn't slept at all. "I think I should go for a walk. I know it's not the best weather, but I think I need some fresh air."

Isobel looked out the window with concern. "It's drizzling, but we can go for a walk, I suppose," she said with a tentative smile.

It was definitely not walking weather, but Adele couldn't sit there having her mind picked apart at the moment. "I think I need to stretch my legs."

"I am sure Lysander has some umbrellas," Isobel said and went downstairs. It was a mad idea going for a walk, but Adele would go mad if she stayed in the house right now— she needed to breathe.

Lysander's man managed to produce two umbrellas and a coat for Adele from somewhere. They stepped out onto the wet, gray street and slowly walked toward Hyde Park. The streets were completely deserted, with only the odd cart or carriage going past.

"Are you sure you don't want to go for a carriage ride instead?" Isobel asked.

"No, I think I need some exercise. I feel as though I have been sitting for days on end."

"Where is Lysander?"

Adele tried to think. "He is in the house somewhere, probably his study. He might have gone to the club—I'm not sure."

They walked in silence for a while. "It is surprisingly nice to go for a walk in this weather—it is as if you have London all to yourself, with everyone being shut away in their houses."

"We explored Venice in the rain and it made it even more memorable, I think." There were some muddy patches that needed to be carefully treated, but Adele appreciated the fresh and brisk air, and the open space. There were no birds singing and the whole city was quiet. "I wonder if it will be a difficult spring this year."

"Adele, why don't you come and stay at my house for a while," Isobel suggested. "There is no reason you must stay at Lysander's. If you are having difficulties getting along, it might be best for all if you come stay with me. You know I have plenty of room."

Adele thought it over for a second. "As much as I appreciate the offer, it is unnecessary; we are not being disagreeable."

"Something has happened," Isobel said disbelievingly.

"No, we have, on the whole, been getting on fine—perhaps better than we ever have. I am just in a funny temper today. I am sorry; I'm not the best company. I think I might lie down for a while when we return; perhaps I might be able to rest."

*

Lysander could hear her coming—that determined march Isobel had when trouble was coming his way. He'd hear it all his life.

"What have you done?" she demanded as the door to his study forcefully swung open.

"I have done nothing," he defended himself, but he knew what his aunt was referring to. Adele looked awful when she'd come down to breakfast in the morning. She'd avoided his eyes and they'd eaten in complete silence. Naturally, his aunt had assumed he'd done something horrible—perhaps he had.

"Nothing? Adele looks like a shadow, stalking the corners. What did you say to her?" Isobel demanded in an even stronger voice.

Lysander looked out the window. "I didn't say anything," he said after a while. Perhaps it wasn't a bad thing that Isobel knew what had happened, because he felt out of his depth—he had since the moment he'd brought Adele back, but more so now. "I took her to the opera last night and we ran into Lord Alterstrong."

"And that cow Cassandra?"

"Yes."

"And you told Adele about your history with Cassandra?"

"No. Adele inferred it. Cassandra was her usual self—slightly familiar. And she's not a cow."

"Yes, she is—you were just never able to see it."

165

He gave her a hard look for her ungenerosity—which he knew had been targeted toward Cassandra, even when they were young.

"Adele reacted…" he said with a forceful flurry of his hand.

"Why do you insist on making her suffer so?" Isobel said with exasperation.

"I don't insist on making her suffer," he said sharply, denying the accusation. "I have never sought to make Adele suffer—"

"But somehow you always manage," Isobel broke in.

"Then tell me, Isobel, what I can do to end her suffering, because I don't know what to do," he said sharply.

"Let her go."

Lysander brought his gaze back to his desk, settling on the sterling silver inkpot. His shoulders sank, but the tension would still not relent.

"Let her go to Devon—let her come to my house. You don't deal well together. Let her go."

"I am not holding her here. If she wants to leave, I will not stop her, but she wishes to stay."

"I cannot believe you, Lysander. I have just come from spending the morning in her company and she is not thriving in your care."

He hated every moment of this discussion, but he was also glad he had someone he could mention his concerns to—Harry wouldn't be receptive or understanding of this conversation and certainly not his concerns for Adele's welfare. "There is a certain matter we have agreed to conduct within the remaining confines of this marriage," he said in a calm, low tone.

"Matter?"

"A matter of …" he couldn't find the right word, "procreation."

Isobel gasped. "Are you lying with her?"

He didn't answer. Groaning loudly in dismay, Isobel paced sharply around the room. "Lysander, I ... Why would you do this? You would wilfully make her suffer for your need for an heir?"

"It is something she has requested," he said, hating the accusation laid at his feet. "She wishes for a child—someone to care for—someone to fill her future. I couldn't deny her."

Isobel closed her eyes. "I am speechless, Lysander. You must see the foolhardiness of this venture. You are reducing her to a shell."

"It serves us both. She is not as fragile as you believe."

"And she is not as strong as you believe."

"Then I will leave it up to Adele to make choices for herself. She is free to leave if she wants to."

"Does she know that?"

"If she doesn't, I will tell her."

Isobel gave him another pointed, accusing look before leaving and he felt her departure like a lightening of atmospheric pressure. Isobel saw all his faults and all his intentions, but he truly didn't intend on Adele's suffering, and what he said was true: if there was any way he could end or diminish her suffering, he would. Providing her with a child was in that vein of intent, but it might be costing too much, he conceded.

*

Adele looked a bit brighter when he saw her in the afternoon—her cheeks had a bit more color. Having stewed on his conversation with Isobel before lunch, he'd decided he needed to conduct a candid discussion with her. If she truly sought to leave, he would help her do so—heir or no. He wasn't prepared to insist if she suffered in the process.

He wasn't sure about how he felt about her leaving. If she left before they created an heir, it would mean some requirements for his future, but he wasn't callous enough to injure her for it.

Searching the house, he found her in the dining room, arranging flowers. She had her back to the door and her hair was up, revealing the back of her slim neck and its pale, smooth skin. For a second, he had an urge to touch her, feel her warm skin under his fingers, but he distracted himself, and her, by clearing his throat. Turning at the sound, she had some flower he couldn't name between her dainty fingers.

"Isobel is concerned that you are not thriving here," he said. Adele turned back to the vase and pushed the stem into the collection. "She feels that perhaps you are better away from here."

Turning back to him, she leaned back on the side of the table. The outline of her legs becoming visible underneath the material of her dress and he had another image that served to distract him.

Her gaze was uncomfortable as she considered him; he felt the pressure of it, but there was no discernible judgment in it. "If you wish to leave, I will arrange it for you—anywhere you wish to go, Devon, Isobel's. I can even get you a cottage somewhere if you wish—just tell me what you want."

"I want a child," she said quietly.

"As you wish," he said and nodded, withdrawing from the room. His heart was beating strongly and his hands sweating, and he had to get out of the room. She wished to stay. A light feeling washed through him—one he couldn't identify, but he was pleased, it seemed.

Returning to his study, he sat down in his chair. The house was quiet again. Somewhere he could hear one of the servants moving around, or perhaps Adele. Somehow it felt like a storm had passed and things had returned to normal— perhaps it was a bit lighter outside as well, he thought as he stared out of the window.

Chapter 22

LYSANDER WAS FEELING RESTLESS the next day. It was a bright but cold day and he felt hemmed in. He considered going to his club, but it was a bit early and Harry was away, which was fine, because for some reason, he didn't really want to see Harry today. But he wanted to do something.

Adele had looked better when she'd come down in the morning. He knew she was in the parlor and after putting down the book of accounts he was supposed to be reviewing, he decided to seek her out, seeking distraction and diversion, and wondered if it would suit her as well.

She looked up from her book as he entered the room and he smiled uncomfortably. "There is an Egyptian exhibition at the British Museum—apparently, there are some recently discovered pieces on display at the moment. Everyone is talking about them, I hear. I thought I would go see what all the fuss was about. Would you like to accompany me?"

There was something about her scrutiny that made him self-aware. There wasn't judgment in her eyes that he could see, but still there was something that made him a little cautious around her.

"I have noticed that you have an interest in intrepid explorers," she said.

"I used to," he admitted. As a boy, he'd wanted to be an explorer and the discoveries in Egypt had always had a grasp on his imagination, but he'd put those dreams aside a long time ago.

"Are you going now?"

"Yes," he said, again with a sense of imposition insisting an immediate response.

"I would love to," she said, putting her book aside.

"I will call the carriage around."

As she retreated to her room for a moment, he waited downstairs, until her return in a blue dress, which caught his attention for a moment, particularly her slim waist, accentuated through the sharp tailoring of the dress. A matching hat graced her head, pinned slightly off-centre. She looked elegant and alluring.

Holding the door open for her, he assisted her into the carriage for the short journey to the British Museum, where she placed her hand in the crook of his arm as they walked up the wide stairs to the Museum's entrance.

"I haven't been here since I was a girl," she said. "My governess used to take me."

"My governess would never hazard taking me in public," he said with a smirk.

She smiled. "No, I was a good girl. My governess took me all around London; she believed in teaching history with examples. We went to the Tower, to the Roman Wall. She even took me to fields where battles had been fought—not that there was anything to see. Looking back, I think her enthusiasm for history was a little excessive."

"I was a naughty child," he confessed and pulled away, smiling as he turned back to her, giving her a conspiratorial look. "My governesses would leave in exasperation."

"I don't believe you were that bad," Adele challenged.

"I saw my fair share of room corners."

"You could not have been too wild; you did secure a place at Oxford."

"Through excessive pledging and pleading by my father."

*

Adele couldn't really see him as the naughty child he described. It was so different from the man she knew—the forbidding, sullen and distant man. A frown settled on her features as she realized it had been her and their marriage that had brought the darker perspective to him—the deep disappointment and knowledge that he wouldn't get what he wanted out of life. She felt sadness fill her again, after she'd worked so hard to find her equilibrium again.

"I always thought I would visit Egypt," he said wistfully. "I might still."

"Will you? I've always thought visiting Cairo would be romantic."

"Romantic? Hot, foreign and crowded."

"You are such a complete Englishman, aren't you? Unless it is gray and raining, you don't feel at home. I am more of an intrepid traveler than you are, I think."

"Did you like India?"

"Yes," she said. "It was so very different."

"Even the crowds."

"They were a bit confronting, I admit, but I managed. I loved the mornings in India, when it was cooler and the sun was rising to the peacock cries."

"We have peacocks here."

"Yes, but they seem to fit better in India."

"You wish to travel more?"

"Yes. I think I will take a leaf from my governess' book and teach my child in real surroundings." She watched as his face clouded over momentarily. "Do you want a child?" she asked after a while.

"Honestly, I hadn't thought about it much beyond the requirements of my station." He grew more serious.

"And while this child will provide me with an heir—in truth, I've seen it more as your child."

"Don't you wish any part in raising it?"

"Do you wish me to?"

It hadn't actually been a question she'd considered. She, too, had seen it as her child, to be taken away to wherever her new home would be. "A child is always benefitted by the influence of its father."

"Are they? Isobel's children don't seem to suffer from their father's absence."

"No, that is true. They are wonderful and she has done an admirable job raising them." Adele thought back to her own father and his distance and distraction. He'd loved her, she knew, and provided her with the best money could buy. He had paid an absolute fortune to secure her a marriage with the right station and society—securing her own misery in the process. In hindsight, it hadn't been a decision that had provided her with anything of value and it had been his own elevation her father had achieved above all else.

Adele's mind returned to the question at hand: would Lysander make a better father—enough to make her want his involvement with the raising of this child? "I cannot believe you don't want children."

"I never said I didn't; I just hadn't spent a great deal of time considering it."

Their conversation was stopped when they arrived at the room holding the new Egyptian discoveries. The room was large and white, with enormous windows along one side of the wall, high above their head. "Perhaps I should go to Egypt," Lysander said as he surveyed a set of pottery from the collection borrowed from the Exposition Universelle. "Would you go to Egypt if you had the chance?"

"In a heartbeat."

173

An Absent Wife

"Traipsing all over the world with a child in tow?"

"Why not?"

"I am glad my mother isn't alive to hear you."

*

They spent two hours walking through the museum, exploring all sorts of exhibitions from ancient worlds covering the entire globe—ancient weapons, to miniature heads, to Mayan carvings. After returning for lunch at home, Adele retreated to her room to rest. Her mind turned over the things he'd said during their excursion.

Lying in bed, she heard Lysander leaving the house, likely to spend time at his club. The house grew completely quiet with his absence.

She had liked spending time with him today. It had been a little like their time in Venice, when they were exploring something together. But her sadness was still there, under the surface, whenever she thought of him and the things they'd been through.

Supper was a muted affair and Adele felt a little stifled in her tight dress and corset, feeling a certain nervousness as she knew he would come to her tonight. She just knew and would be highly surprised if he didn't. There was a silence between them and a sense of anticipation filling the air.

Adele could hardly keep herself still as she waited after having retreated to her room once her untouched desert had been cleared. Having removed her dress, she'd slipped into her nightgown. Normally, she loved this time of day, when her corset came off and she could be free for a while— the time that was completely her own between undressing and sleeping—but tonight he would be joining her and it would be their time, not hers.

She started slightly when he knocked, even though she expected his appearance. Opening the door quietly, he

174

stepped inside. He'd taken his jacket and vest off somewhere, leaving him in a crisp, white shirt. Adele stood at the side of the bed, leaning on the post, feeling heat and anticipation coursing through her body. His eyes were dark and they reflected the light from the candles, making them sparkle as he moved. He looked handsome as he approached her. Her breath caught.

He reached for her, touching the side of her face. "Do you want me here tonight?"

"Yes," she said, a little more breathy than normal.

He looked uncertain for a moment, then slowly leaned down and kissed her. Adele felt the kiss reverberate through her body and she stepped closer, crossing the space between them. His hands gently traveled down the side of her neck and along her shoulders. The familiar taste of him suffused her mind, driving her to seek more.

As the kiss broke, he pulled her to him, moving his mouth to the side of her neck. His breath was heavy in her ear and she was taken over by the feel of his body pressed to hers. It felt as though it had been too long since they'd been like this—these stolen moments when they could forget everything else, and the unpleasantness that had to be dealt with outside of this little sanctuary.

Quick thoughts of Cassandra stole into her consciousness, but she pushed them out. These were her moments—they might be all she'd ever have of him and she wasn't going to let all the mess intrude.

He kissed her again and she let him explore her mouth, urging him to join her on the bed. Adele moaned as the weight of him descended on her, flaring the heat deep in her belly. She wanted more friction as his knee sought entry to the space between hers.

Sitting back, he gently tugged the string that kept the neckline of her nightgown together, as if he was unwrapping

175

a gift. The sides gave way, revealing her breasts which ached for his touch. His fingertips ran down along her collarbone to the mound of her breast and the tight bud that sought attention.

She wanted to move her thigh to get him closer to her center, but his weight kept her pinned where she was. She tugged at his shirt to access his warm smooth skin underneath, feeling the muscles of his back and the flair as his lower back gave way to the firm curves of his backside.

She didn't think she could wait; she wanted him now, but he wasn't yet willing to indulge her. He kissed her again, his tongue stroking hers, along her teeth and lips— lush and teasing, but it wasn't the only part of him she wanted inside her. Distressingly, he seemed to be slowing down. He rolled over to his side, with his free hand moving down to explore her breast.

Adele swallowed hard as the palm of his hand molded the weight of her breasts and his fingers teased the sensitive bud, which shot spears of intense shocks through her. Closing her eyes to them, she was further disturbed when the teasing fingers were replaced with the warm tip of his tongue, then the full teasing of his mouth as it closed around her over-sensitized bud, making her moan in want and driving tension. His tongue whirled around the tense bud as his hand took to traveling lower, toward her core. She couldn't breathe as his fingers reached the sensitive nub at her sex and her legs parted at the touch. The sensation was too much, making her feel she was losing control of her own body. Two fingers pushed into her core, massaging her insides to the point of complete undoing. Powerful waves of pleasure washed through her as he worked his fingers in and out of her, urging her to arch up into the intense release he wrought in her.

"Hmm," he said with appreciation as she pulsed around his fingers. Leaning over her, he kissed her again and she sought the connection eagerly, feeling sheer anticipation as he worked to release the belt holding him tightly confined in his breeches.

He slid smoothly between her thighs and inside her, groaning as he sank fully into her. The overwhelming sensations stole her ability to breathe and she could only suffer through the onslaught of feelings and the sense of fullness. Her hips moved with him as he withdrew and pushed back. She felt she couldn't take any more, but she couldn't stop either. This felt like her purpose and if it killed her for lack of breath, so be it.

Her passage started convulsing around him almost immediately and his thrusts kept the convulsions going almost to the point of pain, then a powerful release shook through her again, the urgency of it clamping down on her chest and lungs as her heart beat powerfully.

When she finally drew breath, it was a great big sob and all tension started to drain away from her body. Lysander had stilled on top of her, recovering as well. Reaching down slowly, he kissed her further—slow, sweet kisses that teased more than demanded. The feel of his lips was playful and light, then he kissed her eyelids before rolling off her onto his back, his chest moving with his heavy breaths.

She missed his warmth, even though her body was heated beyond reason. She missed his touch, not quite wanting it to be over. Turning on her side, she watched him as he lay on his back with his eyes closed, recovering his breath. He was utterly beautiful, looking disheveled and undone. She wanted to trace her finger along the outlines of his face, but tightened her hand to stop herself.

When things changed, she would miss this. She wasn't sorry for having experienced this or her own reaction to him, but she would miss this a great deal.

Chapter 23

ADELE WAS ON PINS AND needles, unable to sit still. Her bleeds were supposed to have started yesterday and yet there was nothing. Now that her hope had built up, she would be devastated if it turned out to be false.

She would wait another day, she told herself. In the meantime, she needed a distraction to keep her mind from worrying, except she couldn't really settle on anything. It was too rainy for taking a walk and she was too agitated to do anything sedate, like embroidering. She didn't think she'd ever experienced time moving so slowly.

It was true that she was afraid of letting her mind wander to the joys and requirements of a baby, or even the pregnancy, to be disappointed after making extensive plans for a new life with a baby. She gave a silent prayer yet again, hoping it was true.

Lysander was out of the house. She wanted to share her worries with him, but would refrain from it until she was a little more certain—one day overdue didn't constitute confirmation of any kind. Her thoughts turned to him more generally. It was possible that they had achieved what they'd set out to do in a surprisingly quick time. Adele would miss the nights they'd spent together in the attempt to bring this about—but they had also wreaked havoc on her peace of mind. She hoped her body would readjust and she could focus her attention on this child. This child meant that she would finally be leaving this marriage behind and she was glad. It had been nothing but trouble for both of them and now it was over. She'd been sad about that state of her marriage for much too long—now she would be excited about this baby and the future filled with joy and childhood.

"Please, please, please be true," she whispered to herself as she paced back and forth.

*

Lysander had just sat down to breakfast when he heard Adele bound down the stairs like an over-excited girl. A spike of concern flashed through him, that something was wrong, but it wasn't a distressed and crying woman who greeted him, it was Adele looking not far off an over-excited child. Her cheeks were rosy and her eyes were bright, and she was smiling widely. He hadn't seen her like this since he agreed to take her around Venice.

As she marched to him, he felt slightly confused as he rose from the chair. She marched straight into his arms, in an unexpected embrace and he almost had to brace himself against the force of it.

"It's been four days," she stated as she stood against him.

"Four days since...?"

She cast a wary eye at Jamieson, who stood in the corner overseeing the breakfast service. His man discreetly cleared his throat and went to check on something in the kitchen. "Four days since ... my bleeds were supposed to start," she said in a whisper.

"Oh," he said with his eyebrows rising. The news had taken him completely by surprise—not that it should. "Oh, I see." He placed his hand gently on the small of her back, noting how slight she felt.

"Thank you," she said, reaching up to kiss him. The kiss was also unexpected and lasted perhaps a little longer than it should. Then she pulled away from the kiss and from him.

"Isn't it the most exciting news?" She walked over to the side table where breakfast was being served. "Apparently, I must eat well. I should consult with Isobel if there is anything I should eat that will be strengthening for the baby."

"Have you spoken to Doctor Petersen?"

"Not yet. I thought I would have him call today. I wish it wasn't raining. This rain is driving me to distraction, keeping me cooped inside—on such a day; I want to tell the world. I don't mind telling you that the wait over the last few days have been absolutely excruciating."

Lysander realized that she'd been holding this news for several days; waiting for the veracity of it. He'd had no idea. Adele dropped some ham on her plate, along with two eggs, a slice bread and some asparagus stalks.

"I shall eat fruit, lots and lots of fruit," she said. "Perhaps not fish ... unless it comes from good, clean waters."

He had never experienced Adele quite like this— excited and distracted. She was chattering.

"There is so much I need to do," she continued. "I need a perambulator, and a feeding chair. I need toys, and clothes. The list is endless."

"And a miniature traveling trunk," he said, referring to the conversation they'd had at the British Museum. Adele gave him a confused look and returned her attention to eating.

"Perhaps even a dog," she said more quietly. She didn't pick up on the reference to the discussion they'd had about her wish to travel with the child—show it the world. She was too distracted with the future. Lysander felt a bit as if she was sweeping the past away, including the discussions they'd had. He was clearly not in the picture of her musings, because she wasn't asking his opinion—she was planning for herself, which had always been their intent. It was just difficult to witness, he discovered, being set aside—exactly like he had done to her.

"If we shall live in the country, we could even have a pony," she continued, her eyes sparkling with a mischievous smile. His eyes rolled that her idea of mischievous included getting a pony.

Lysander needed a drink, something strong—even if it was only eight in the morning. Her 'we's' didn't include him—he was to stay here in this empty house, with his club, his evening entertainments—and Evie. The thought of Evie made him feel despondent. No, he didn't think he could abide Evie's company anymore, no matter what happened.

"I think I will go to the club this morning," he said. Adele gave him a passing nod in acknowledgment, but her mind immediately returned to her planning. He wasn't even sure she'd actually absorbed what he'd said.

Stepping out on the street, he noted how stifled he had felt in his house. Although he was glad for Adele's excitement and enthusiasm, he also felt confronted by it. At least Isobel wouldn't be accusing him of making her suffer now, because she clearly wasn't.

There was hardly anyone out this time of the morning; he rarely saw the world outside his bedroom this time of the day either. When he arrived, the club was practically deserted as well—just the odd sprinkling of elderly gentlemen for whom this was likely midday. So he was conferring with this set now, he thought grimly. Taking a seat in a deserted group of chairs, he grabbed a newspaper and ordered a whiskey. The butlers at the club were discreet enough not to bat an eyelid as his request for hard liquor this time of the morning.

He tried to read, but he couldn't seem to engage his mind properly. After a few moments of trying, he set the paper aside and crossed his fingers in his lap.

When Adele had come bounding down the stairs this morning, his marriage was effectively over. This had been the event he'd wished for, coming up to a decade. Yet somehow, it didn't feel like the celebration it was. With this child and a simple petition and he would be free—free not to have a wife. As for the child, a boy would be preferable, but a girl wasn't a disaster in this day and age. And he would return to the life he wanted, finally free of Adele.

He would also be free of a woman who waited for him in the evenings, who gave so sweetly of her body. He had to close his eyes as the thoughts of their nights together washed over him, making him tense and tighten. He would miss the evenings in Adele's company. He'd never experienced the like before, and he suspected he wouldn't again. He'd even started preferring spending the evenings at home, instead of seeking entertainment and diversion amongst London's society. And now she was leaving.

"The harpy's driven you to drink this early in the morning?" Harry said as he sat down heavily in the chair across from him. Lysander had been too absorbed in his own thoughts to notice his friend's arrival. Smiling grimly at his friend's comment, he acknowledged that it was true; she had driven him to drink, but for the exact opposite reason to what Harry thought.

Lysander held up his glass and took a swig. "What's she done now?" Harry's derisive tone didn't even attempt to hide what he thought of her, and Lysander had to take some responsibility as he'd cultivated his friend's disregard for his wife long before she ran off and deserted her marriage.

"Adele is pregnant," he said.

Harry gave a quick nod. "Congratulations," he said. "In that case, I will join you." He attracted the attention of one of the butlers and ordered himself a glass as well. "Now you can divorce her."

"Yes," Lysander said, but it clearly didn't hold the level of enthusiasm that Harry was expecting. "But should I? If she is with child, she needs protection."

"Protection? We're not exactly living in the dark ages—besides, she is a grown woman, capable of taking care of herself. And if you are to worry about her comfort just because she is breeding, then what is the difference then to worrying for her comfort when she is nursing, or has a young child. When will it end?"

Lysander rubbed the smooth skin of his chin as if there was stubble there.

"No," Harry continued. "Better to do this now. Set her up in comfort if you wish—if it makes you feel more at ease, but there is no reason to extend this horror of a marriage. You are a good man, but you have suffered long enough. Divorce her now, have the petition prepared. I knew she would be trying to ingratiate herself with you. This is a ploy, Lysander."

Frowning, Lysander took yet another swig of his whiskey. Harry's opinion of Adele was unjustly harsh, but he knew Harry wouldn't change his mind if he tried to explain, and would cite it as further evidence of her attempts to manipulate him, when that truth was the Adele likely wanted this divorce as much as Harry did.

"Have the petition prepared today," Harry said firmly.

Chapter 24

AFTER SUPPER, LYSANDER retreated to his study, feeling pensive and restless. He wasn't entirely sure he was ready for this change that had come on so quickly. He tried to tell himself that he should be glad that he was now free and released from a burden that had held him for a very long time, but it left him feeling agitated.

He couldn't sit here and sulk, he decided. The house had that stifling quality again and it set his nerves on edge. Neither did he know where Harry was that night; he hadn't thought to inquire earlier.

Lysander headed out of the house. He didn't quite know where he was headed, but any entertainment would do. After arriving at his club, he fell in with the group of an acquaintance—a young, ambitious man freshly from Oxford, who had tried to befriend him in the past—impressed with his title and wealth. Lysander didn't normally associate with the younger, unmarried and carefree men, but he needed diversion and their high spirits were appealing.

After consuming a few whiskeys, mellowness set in and the agitation that had stolen into him started to give. The young men were raucous and before long they ended up at an establishment with women, drinking and gambling—the trifecta of the gentleman's distraction. This particular establishment was French and they made every effort to create merriment, from raucous dancers on a stage with colorful ruffled skirts and undergarments, to bright lights and sumptuous décor—the music fast and loud enough to prevent one from hearing one's own thoughts.

The drinks were flowing and Lysander gave himself over to the atmosphere of the place, forgetting the dour mood he'd left home with.

*

The house was quiet once Lysander had left, leaving Adele to sort out her competing emotions. The baby's existence was possibly the most exciting news she'd ever received, perhaps even competing with the day when she'd been told she was to marry. Thoughts had been racing around her head all day; there was so much that needed doing—needed preparing. She had her whole future to establish.

But there was also a sadness as well, because this was the closing of a chapter, to bring on the next. It wasn't a chapter she was strictly sorry to see closed, as there were years of convoluted feelings involved—most of them negative and detracting, but not all. After convincing herself she had done so, she needed to finally let go of Lysander, which was proving more difficult after the intimacies they'd developed out of necessity just lately.

Their communion, while having the intent of creating this baby, had also had the effect of letting her explore the emotional intimacy she'd always craved. She'd tried to keep it at bay, but had to give up on that idea rather quickly. She liked to think of it as an exorcism to finally deal with the ghost of the man who had inhabited her life in spirit for so long. As for the real man, the man who had come to her each night; she couldn't really afford to think about him. She didn't wish him harm, but it was time to end it all. And that felt right.

Laying down on her bed, she let the sadness of the moment take over and began crying hot, heavy, sobbing tears, knowing she needed to shed these tears. The tension and longing of years filled those tears. Now she needed to let go; she needed to make room for this baby and to clear away the past. She would mourn the passing of that phase in her life for one night, along with the unfulfilled hopes and dreams she'd carried for so long, but then she will put it aside and focus on the bright future. She cried bitterly for a few hours then fell asleep, feeling she'd released a burden from her soul.

*

Lysander returned to a quiet house. He was drunk—not as drunk as he had been, but still drunk—and bitter. The only thing he really wanted was to go up to Adele's room and be welcomed into her arms, to revel in the sweet peace and acceptance he'd received there. She'd never accept him in this state, but his concerns weren't exclusively or realistically for this moment—but perhaps he needed to be in this state to be honest with himself. He'd found something in his wife's urgent touch—something he hadn't quite found elsewhere. And now it was being taken away—its purpose achieved. He had served his duty, and now he was being put out to pasture like an old horse.

That wasn't entirely true, but it was how he felt, even though he was the one divorcing her. Yet again, she was causing strife and trouble in his life and consciousness—he should be glad to be rid of her.

Leaning back, he undid the cravat that stifled his movement and free breathing. He longed to be touched, longed to be accepted into her room and into her bed. The heady desire had been there all night, underneath everything, running through from moment to moment, like the mist of smoke that clung to everything in the gentlemen's establishment he'd been to that night.

But his reason for access into her bed and her body was moot now. The very practical reason for it in the first place was gone and now he was left with burning desire in his loins, which he couldn't successfully drink away. Everything about Adele was cruel, and the fact that she'd never intended it made it crueller still.

Running his fingers along the glossy wood of his desk, he let the sensations of touch reverberate up his fingers. This desire would drive him mad. Pulling his fingers back, he tightened his fist, trying to dissipate the feel of the touch. Whenever he closed his eyes, his desire gave him images to torture him. He drank some more—at some point, the drink would take over and he would feel nothing.

*

The stark and painful morning arrived with suddenness. Having slept in his chair, Lysander's neck ached. His body was tense and sore, and his head screamed its protest at the way he'd treated his body the previous night. The sun shone straight into his eyes through the window and he tried to find an effective way of blocking it out, but failed.

Eventually, he had to heave himself out of his chair and labored upstairs to flop down on his bed. He slept a few hours longer, still dressed, before waking again and grudgingly sitting up. His head still ached; the world was still intent on his punishment, it seemed.

After washing and shaving, he dressed in a fresh shirt. As had become customary of late, he would leave the house again, seek out his club and the comforting surroundings of the all-male establishment. He needed distance to get a better perspective, being driven by desire at the moment, knowing it would lead him astray if he let it. He wouldn't be the first man for whom it had happened, although he'd guarded well against it until now. It was as if a beast had been let loose in him and it was screaming for what he wanted—irrespective of what was prudent and logical. Prudent and logical didn't include developing a sharp desire for his wife just as he was divorcing her—the one who had deeply embarrassed him, played havoc with his reputation, not to mention his peace of mind, and made him travel across the world in a ruse of deceit. He needed to step back, let a cooler head emerge—he needed to get perspective.

Breakfast was long gone by the time he finally made it out of his room and he left the house without much delay. It was a sunny day outside, just to annoy him and his aching head with its infernal, blinding sunshine.

Harry was at the club, sitting in their usual place— the creatures of habit that they were.

"Christ, you look awful. What is she doing to you?"

"Driving me to distraction—literally."

"And it seems you were distracted."

"Severely."

Lysander ordered tea, but didn't bother to attempt the newspaper with its small print and uninteresting stories.

"Have you had the papers drawn up?" Harry asked and Lysander tsked in annoyance to which Harry noted his disagreeableness. He had sent a letter requesting the divorce petition papers, but he didn't want to talk about it. "None of this is my doing," Harry pointed out.

"Then don't speak about things you know nothing about," Lysander snapped. Harry was surveying him now. Lysander had been downright rude and he knew it, but what he'd said was true to his feelings—Harry's constant negativity and misconception wasn't helping. Lysander wondered if he should leave, but he really didn't have anywhere to go. "I'm sorry," he said after a while. "I am out of sorts today and my head aches like there are imps hammering on it."

"Yes well, we have all suffered from the effects of over-indulgence." Harry returned his attention to his paper and Lysander felt both ashamed and glad, knowing his friend was watching out for his interests, and to some extent, he needed it, because he was getting lost in the intricacies of the situation and his rather powerful and unfortunate desire for his wife.

Chapter 25

A LARGE ENVELOPE ARRIVED from the solicitor a week later. Lysander knew what it was. Placing it down on the desk in his study, it felt heavy in his hands. He pinched the bridge of his nose, trying to rub away the ache in his head. His body was aching as well, from the constant evenings out drinking. When the sun came down, he just couldn't stay in the house.

Annoyed at his own hesitance, he reached for the solicitor's envelope and ripped it open. The parchment inside was crisp and the writing neat. He read through the petition and everything was as he expected.

The space at the bottom requiring his signature stared blankly at him. Slowly he picked up his pen, placed it in the ink well and brought it over to the paper. His hand shook as it hovered over the paper.

If he signed this, it would start the process—a process that would probably go quite quickly. Adele's actions were known far and wide, so it wouldn't take much convincing to have a judge sign it—unless Adele contested it, which he doubted she would do. She seemed too distracted to worry about the dissolution of their marriage. She hadn't even discussed the provisions he would give her. Technically, he didn't have to give her anything—being divorced meant she only had non-marital income or wealth to rely on, which was practically nothing.

Lysander would provide her with sufficient funds to live and raise the child. As opposed to some other divorced husbands, he didn't wish to see her suffer and destitute as a consequence of the ending of the marriage. He wasn't entirely sure what her plans were, but he could afford almost any circumstance she chose.

The pen still hovered over the space where his signature was to go. He felt intense pressure and his thoughts whirled around as to the implications of signing the petition. He needed to sign this to achieve what they both wanted. He would also be signing away the intimacy they'd had and the desire that still gripped him with enough force to drive him out of the house every night.

A drop of ink fell from the hovering pen, spreading like a spider's web across the paper. His hand just didn't seem to want to lower. There was such a finality in the act— signing his marriage away. To his own surprise, he just couldn't bring himself to sign it at the moment. Perhaps he was just feeling a little off-color from his nights out, and a little sentimental. This is what they both wanted; he should just sign the petition and let this pass without fanfare, complying with everyone's expectations. No-one, not even himself, would understand why he wasn't signing it.

"I am going to go out for a while," he heard Adele's voice from the doorway. Quickly and discreetly he shoved the parchment under a pile of documents, hoping that her attention wasn't drawn to his action.

"Oh?"

"There is a perambulator maker in Marylebone that is very respected. I know it is early days, but he apparently requires much notice. I thought I would go see what samples they have available."

"Pardon?"

"A perambulator—a small carriage for taking a small child for walks."

"I see. Of course. I will escort you." He hadn't meant to offer his assistance; it had just come out.

She nodded in acknowledgment, obviously not expecting company either. "Jamieson is having the carriage brought around."

"Good," Lysander said, standing from his chair. He suspected that part of the reason why he was eager to take his wife to see this perambulator-maker was to alleviate himself for the moment of the unpleasant task confronting him. He clearly wasn't in the mood to deal with it and sign the petition.

When the carriage pulled in on the sidewalk outside the house, Lysander helped Adele and joined her on the opposing seat. Her hands were neatly placed in her lap and she was watching out the window. His eyes traveled to her flat stomach, stiffly braced by a corset. "Should you be wearing a corset?"

"It is not as tight as I normally have it. But I will stop wearing it after a month or so. I may not be fashionable, but then who will see me?"

Lysander frowned. Adele's statement indicated her own intent, and it was obviously living reclusively to some degree. Once he signed the petition hiding on his desk and it was approved, he had no say in what she did. It was a challenging notion as he'd had complete say and an expectation that she would comply with his wishes; although that had to some degree been negated when she ran off to India. He wasn't a man who derived satisfaction from enforcing his will, but it had become an expectation.

He wanted to ask her what she was planning, but he couldn't bring himself to do it, making him wonder at his own inability to face the future. Perhaps because the future that was coming his way didn't now seem like the light and carefree time he'd used to envision. The truth was that he would worry about Adele, even though it would no longer be his right or his concern. But his child would also be in her

193

hands, which meant he would worry more. It was his right to insist he keep the child, and the law would support him, but he couldn't do that to her—and what would he do with a child? His life as a carefree bachelor would hardly be conducive to raising a child. Adele would be in the throes of motherhood and child-rearing and he would be... He couldn't even really image his own future—days reading the newspaper at the club, afternoons going over his investments and evenings in the arms of some woman of Evie's ilk. That had been his life before and what he'd worked definitively to defend, but somehow it seemed to have lost its appeal.

"Shall you go to Egypt?" she asked, breaking into his disturbing thoughts. Lysander jumped at the chance for distraction and was also pleased that she remembered part of the discussion they'd had during their day at the British Museum.

"I haven't thought further on it."

"I think you should."

"And shall you?"

"Go to Egypt?"

"With the child."

"Maybe," she said, smiling. "The child will be too young for a few years yet, but when it's old enough, I would like to do a few trips. Perhaps not somewhere as exotic as Egypt, but maybe France—possibly Spain or Italy." Her gaze returned to the window and he felt a moment of impatience losing her attention. "Do you think you shall remarry?"

"No."

"No? Why not."

"I will have my heir."

"Is that the only benefit of a marriage?" she said, watching him intently.

"I have been married if you recall," he said. "Technically I still am. I think we can both agree that I have certain deficiencies as a husband."

"But you cannot judge all marriages by the failure of ours. Our marriage had too many strikes against it to ever have been successful."

He used to believe so, but of late, he'd started to wonder if things couldn't have been different if he'd released his anger earlier. "Did it? Isn't the construct of our marriage typical?"

"Perhaps it was just the nature of the two people involved that did not match. You cannot judge the institution by the failings of this one. You should find someone you're happy with. I wish that for you." It looked as if there was something else she wanted to add, but was holding back.

"How disparate are our natures, though? When we are in the same space, we deal quite well together." He looked out the window for a moment. "When we were intimate, we dealt extraordinarily together." Didn't she know that? Were her experiences with Mr Ellingwood just as profound? He felt a wall of anger rush through him at the thought. He wanted their intimacy to be as unique to her as it had been to him. He cleared his throat. "The point being that perhaps we were never that badly matched. Perhaps I am not well-suited for marriage."

"I don't believe that."

"You are the one who has suffered most from my lack of matrimonial suitability. I have come to realize that it was not you that was the shortcoming in this marriage. You never did anything wrong."

"Except to run off to India," Adele said in an attempt to lighten the conversation.

"After so many years, who would truly say it wasn't understandable. I left you alone. Eventually, a man would come along; turn your head."

*

Adele's concern washed over her features. She'd always wanted to hear him say those things, but now that he was, she wasn't sure she wanted it anymore. Perhaps they were better off not clearing this all up and continuing as they were. This analysis in the aftermath may not serve either of them.

"Will you marry again?" he asked.

"I have no intention to at the moment. I think my attention will be with the child for quite a while to come, but eventually, if I have the opportunity, then yes."

Lysander looked away; she saw the muscle in his jaw tensing. She wasn't quite sure where his thoughts were at right now. He seemed to be analyzing the past and the things that had made their marriage the disaster that it was. If she were completely honest, she didn't want to think about it anymore; she'd spent too much time in her life doing so and she just wanted to leave it behind—yet again.

They arrived at the street where perambulator merchant had his facility. It was a busy main street with many shops. Adele spotted a store across the street which sold fine soaps that she wanted to visit as well, but she might not have the chance now that she had company. She didn't begrudge him coming along—he would be paying for these purchases after all. They hadn't discussed the appropriateness of her purchasing these things for the child while she was still within the confines of this marriage and under his responsibility, for paying her commitment to merchants. Discussing it would mean a broader discussion on the means she would have later. If he was to provide her with means, then it didn't matter if it was spent now or later. If he was not providing her with means, she could likely not afford a perambulator of this quality—but he was here, which meant he was obviously willing to provide these things.

Adele walked into the store, which was more of a workshop than a store. There were a few samples of perambulators, one beautifully crafted contraption in deep mahogany and rich velvet.

"That one is for the Duke and Duchess of Summervale," a man said as he approached them.

"It is quite magnificent."

"Some would say ridiculous, but it's all down to taste," the craftsman said, wiping his hands on his apron.

"Perhaps slightly more than I require," Adele admitted. Lysander walked ahead of her, surveying the workshop and the child-carriages they were building. "Do you have something that is more suited to the country?"

Lysander turned his attention to her, his eyes dark and brooding. She couldn't quite make out if he was giving her a harsh look or not.

Chapter 26

IT WAS RAINING AGAIN AND Adele hated the limits it placed on her. Now that she was pregnant, Lysander would never let her go for a walk in the rain.

Perhaps she had grown accustomed to the country over the years, seemingly having lost her enthusiasm for living in the city. They seemed to have stopped their evening excursions, which honestly wasn't a great loss. She'd been to the opera; it had been a rather traumatic experience and she wasn't exactly hopping to get back in that saddle. Perhaps her agitation also stemmed from the fact that her future was away from here. She supposed it was natural that one started to detach from one's old life when such a drastic change was expected.

But this baby was going to take a long time to grow and she had to be patient. The rain just made it a bit harder.

"He doesn't want me to go, but I am not sending him off somewhere sight unseen," Isobel said, seated behind Adele as she stood by the window staring out at the wet street. Isobel had come to call a short while earlier and they'd taken tea in the parlor.

"Of course you must go."

"Isn't he getting too old to be embarrassed of his mother?" Andrew's securance of a place in Oxford was cause for celebration.

"Does he resent having to leave behind the girl he's developed an attachment to?"

"I suppose, but he is also excited about the things ahead of him. But since I forced him, I suppose he is obliged to act surly. But no matter, off he goes. He can write to the girl and if their attachment survives the separation, then perhaps it is a good match. At least this way, I won't be a grandmother for a few years yet."

"You would make a wonderful grandmother."

"With a young child of my own," Isobel said with a tsk. "You must come over for dinner this week. We must celebrate Andrew's placement."

"Of course."

"I will ask Lysander too."

Adele's smile didn't falter, but it was true, their dealings were a little strained of late. Lysander had become surly as well, and he was away from the house most of the time—to her own relief, admittedly. "I'm sure he would love to."

*

Preparing for the evening at Isobel's, Adele hoped that it would be a nice evening without the awkwardness that had developed between her and Lysander. She could hear him waiting impatiently downstairs through her open bedroom door. He was pacing.

Securing her earring, she rose to leave, taking one last look in the mirror, wondering how long it would take before her belly actually started to show the signs of pregnancy. She hadn't stopped wearing the corset just yet, but it was loosely drawn. It was just so very obvious when she wasn't wearing it, almost indecent—but the child needed space to grow, so the corset had to go.

She smiled at Lysander when she walked down the stairs, but he didn't return the smile. She would have rolled her eyes if she'd been completely unobserved. He changed so very much; they'd gotten on really well for a while, but now they were back to distance and surliness—she supposed she shouldn't be surprised.

The carriage ride over to Isobel's house was silent with the few exceptions of when he enquired about her wellbeing. Isobel was waiting at the door and greeted them both warmly. The familiar traits were evident when Isobel and Lysander stood next to each other, making Adele wonder what traits her child would inherit. She wished this pregnancy would just progress so she could meet her child— this waiting was tiresome.

"Well, luckily, she doesn't seem too harshly affected, but that might change."

"Sorry?" Adele asked as she realized they were talking about her.

"With nausea."

"No, nothing yet."

"Then you are lucky, but it might still come."

They walked into the house and through to the salon, where a footman provided glasses of sherry. Andrew waited for the guests' arrival on one of the sofas, standing as they entered the room.

Lysander and Andrew talked for a while about Oxford and some of Lysander's experiences there. Even though Andrew was attending another school in Oxford, he was nervously absorbing all the information he could. Adele felt a little sorry for him, being sent off to the venerable institutions that represented higher learning at Oxford, with all the tradition and expectations that went with it.

"He should do quite well," Isobel said. "He is not ill-suited to study, but it needs to be topics that interest him, and his interests run to the more practical, like architecture or engineering. He has an endless fascination for the Underground Rail System."

Adele thought back to Lysander's fascination for explorers, a topic that still engaged him if he gave it opportunity to—although far from his actual life now.

"How is Lysander?" Isobel asked as if reading her thoughts.

"I don't know. We seemed to have returned to more tense dealings."

"That is unfortunate."

*

The supper bell rang and they all moved to the dining room, which was handsomely laid out with silver, porcelain and bouquets. Lysander had never really held dinner parties as his wife had never been around to perform the role of hostess. It should perhaps have been something they should have done, but he hadn't thought of it. He had no idea what her skills were, but she seemed to know wifely duties well.

"So when are you departing for Oxford?" Lysander asked.

"On Friday," Andrew said, coloring slightly at the prospect.

"Excellent."

"As Andrew will not be using his room for the next year, I thought Adele could occupy it for a while," Isobel said with cheeriness, watching Andrew to see if he objected. It wasn't Andrew she should be watching, Lysander thought with a frown. His eyes moved to Adele, who was watching between him and Isobel. He didn't like the idea. "As you are divorcing, the idea that Adele live under my roof seems entirely appropriate."

Lysander's eyes narrowed, wondering if Isobel was trying to coerce him by bringing this topic up in front of other people. "I don't think that is necessary."

Isobel's gaze moved squarely to him, a look of concern in her eyes. "Come, nephew, I could use the company and Adele will need calm as the baby grows."

"Our house is much calmer, besides, you are running after a child all day."

"Skills she will have to learn."

Lysander's mood had darkened considerably once the soup was brought in, ending the conversation. He didn't like Isobel's interference, particularly stated in such a public and challenging way.

The meal continued, but Lysander had lost some of his enjoyment of the occasion. Isobel and Adele were discussing the merits of the latest fashion, and even the ice-cream couldn't meet with his approval. Something seemed to strain against the idea of Adele leaving and taking up residence here. On some level, it felt like an insult, but he couldn't quite place the reasoning behind it.

As the dinner finished, Andrew had gone upstairs to collect a book he wanted to discuss, while Adele retreated to the privy.

"Why are you standing in the way, Lysander?" Isobel asked him directly.

"I just don't think it is appropriate that you suggest where my wife should live."

"And as you are getting divorced, perhaps it is not yours to speak for her."

"She is my wife." Lysander temper flared.

"You are getting divorced. You have to let her go now."

Lysander had no response; he just felt anger and entrapment, and unable to explain why the idea of her living here strained so much.

"We are not divorced yet. She is still my wife."

Isobel was watching him in the way she did when she was suspicious of his motives. "Why must you insist on making things difficult for her?"

Again he had no answer. "I don't appreciate interference in my marriage."

"I am trying to prepare her for what is to come, for her life when you are no longer there—not that you ever

202

were, but she needs to start being independent. Can't you see that I am trying to help her?"

Lysander felt trapped. His reaction was extraordinary and, frankly, baseless, but he couldn't help it. He wasn't ready for everything to proceed so quickly and without his initiation.

Adele returned to the room, looking slightly confused. "Alright, maybe I am feeling a little nauseous," she said.

"That is all very normal," Isobel smiled at her.

Andrew returned as well, starting a discussion on theories around the construction of taller buildings. They all retreated to the salon again, where Lysander asked for a whiskey, wondering if he should perhaps seek out more male company once this was over and he had returned Adele safely to the house. He had lost his appetite for discussion and bitterly wished for another whiskey, maybe three.

The evening ended shortly after and Adele moved to the vestibule to dress in her cloak, when Isobel pulled him aside.

"I want her to come and live here, Lysander."

"I am not obliged to take orders from you regarding my wife and child."

"You are being unreasonable and cruel. At some point, you need to start considering the welfare of others ahead of your own, but Adele's shift here is a reasonable course considering what is ahead. If you are seeking to punish her, then you need to stop."

"I am not seeking to punish her," he said against gritted teeth, resenting the accusation.

"Then what are you doing?"

He dismissed her question, tired of having to explain himself. They were not divorced yet; everyone needed to stop trying to force his hand. Things would develop when they were supposed to. What was the point in rushing ahead?

Chapter 27

LYSANDER'S FOUL MOOD STUCK with him as he left the house early the next day. Isobel's suggestion had been creeping around his mind all night. Things were just moving too fast. If Isobel had her way, the carpet would be ripped out from under his feet before he knew what was going on; actually, not the carpet, his wife. He still had some say in his own marriage and he just couldn't understand what this sense of urgency was all about.

He was also a bit disappointed in Adele. If she wanted to leave his house, she could have come to him and spoken her wishes. He wondered if Isobel and Adele had been colluding behind his back—leaving him completely in the dark as to what their intentions were. He didn't like it one bit.

It was too early for alcohol, even for the way he'd been drinking of late. He settled for ordering a tea service when he arrived at the club, joining the elderly gentlemen who frequented the club in the early hours of the morning, before most were even out of their beds. With a huff, Lysander sat down and opened the paper in front of him, but he just couldn't focus. His mind didn't want to settle of late, making him useless in terms of surveying his investments.

He recognized that he was deeply unhappy and unsettled at the moment. Divorce was not turning into the simple thing he'd expected—a celebration of freedom. Things were much more complicated. Then again, Adele hadn't turned out to be the woman he'd thought she was either. This hesitancy he'd developed was robbing him of peace of mind—as was the withdrawal of the welcome into her bed. The idea of making his barring permanent and irretrievable was uncomfortable. The divorce would rob him of a way back there if he chose.

He was hesitating on the divorce because it forbade him from ever again sleeping with his wife, which was ridiculous, but there was truth in it. It sounded callous and immature even to his own ears, but he knew that it wasn't just about the sex—the divorce would end any potential for establishing a relationship with Adele. He stopped himself from saying re-established, because they'd never had one. But they had rubbed along quite well for a while—maybe even to the point where it had been what he thought a marriage could be, and if he let it go now, he was letting go of the very idea of marriage. Contrary to the beliefs he'd professed to Adele a few days back, in practicality, giving up on the institution wholesale wasn't something he was completely embracing, it seemed.

Harry's arrival made Lysander realize that he had no idea how long he'd sat there, musing over his own troubles. "The fog has finally cleared," Harry said as he sat down.

"Has it?" Lysander hadn't even noticed the fog when he'd walked over here this morning.

"Pea soup."

"How is your wife?" Lysander asked.

"Fine, I suppose. She wants to visit her sister in Bournemouth."

Lysander could tell by Harry's tone that he wasn't excited about the idea. While Harry didn't readily profess his love for his wife, it was there, in sufficient quantities to make him apprehensive of her leaving him on his own for a month. "Perhaps the sister could come to visit her here."

"I've suggested that, but Lucinda came here last year and Clara feels it's only right that she go to Bournemouth this year." Harry surveyed his nails for a while. "Evie came to see me."

Lysander's eyes snapped to his friend's, utterly dismayed with this development. Evie had no right to seek out his friends to discuss the state of their affairs.

"She's worried that you are being manipulated."

"And seeking you out would not be an example of the behavior she is so worried about?" Lysander said icily.

"It is just that you seem hesitant to do what is required."

Lysander was too angry to have this discussion. He couldn't believe Evie felt it was her place to interfere in his marriage, particularly when he'd made his views clear. "How is it that everyone seems to think I am incapable of dealing with my own marriage?"

"Because you're not doing what needs to be done."

"Needs to be done in whose mind? Yours? Evie's? Since when do you have a say?"

"That tart is whispering things in your ear."

"She is my wife! I will not have you speaking ill of her!" Lysander roared, loud enough to draw the attention of everyone in my room. "What she whispers in my ear is categorically none of your concern. Is it my business what Clara whispers in your ear?"

"It is if Clara behaves like your wife does."

"You know nothing of my wife."

"Yes, I do. You are the one who seems to have lost all perspective and everyone seems aware of it other than you."

"I've had enough of this," Lysander said, rising from his chair. "Don't ever speak of or about Adele again." Marching out of the room, Lysander waited impatiently for his coat to be brought. He had to get out of there—not even his club was safe anymore. He was running out of places to go.

He'd be damned if he was going to let anyone tell him what to do, and the idea of them sneaking around his back, colluding to force his hand raised pure fury in him. It felt like a clear threat—a threat to his home.

Lysander stopped dead as he walked down the street. He was fighting for his marriage, he realized—fighting Isobel, Harry, Evie, even Adele, to protect his marriage. Clarity finally struck: he didn't want this marriage finished. It was obvious now; he'd been avoiding every step that would bring this marriage closer to its end—the petition papers, Adele's movement to Isobel's, the retreating of intimacy between them. It wasn't just about choices; he wanted this marriage to realize the potential he's discovered it could have.

He had two choices in front of him, a future with a wife and a child, or a future alone with manipulative women like Evie for company, and Harry constantly telling him how lucky he was that he gave away his one opportunity to have a life with his wife and child.

Turning his thoughts to Adele, he saw her in his mind with that rare smile she gave when he'd pleased her, and then to the even sweeter evenings they'd spent together. Looking back, they'd just about had what he'd wanted. He hadn't known it at the time, but things had just about been perfect. Adele was the perfect wife; she was giving, somewhat independent, intelligent and willing to explore new things—her kisses touched places deep in him and her body sent heat flowing along his spine. Why was he giving that up?

Turning toward his house, he realized he needed to talk to her. It was all just so simple. His step was light for the first time in ages, the heaviness that had weighed him down seemed to have lifted—and it solved all the problems.

*

Adele wandered along a deserted path in Hyde Park. The day was finally clearing; the heavy wetness in the air lifting. The weather made for a solitary walk, which is what she preferred, especially now when her thoughts were heavy. Lysander's vitriolic reaction to Isobel's suggestion sat uneasily with her. She couldn't understand his objection and why he wasn't promoting it himself.

Her thoughts were distracted by the sound of the gravel crunching behind her. Someone was coming, apparently in a bit of a hurry, too.

"Adele," Lysander said when she turned around.

"Lysander. I wasn't expecting you here. Has something happened?"

"In a manner of speaking."

"I hope everything is fine," she said with instant concern.

"I went home, but you weren't there. I wanted to have words with you."

"About?"

He looked nervous. "The last few months, as we have spent a considerable amount of time together, it has shown us that this marriage can be tolerable to us both, and as you are now carrying our child, it seems natural that we carry on as we are."

Adele's mouth opened involuntarily. "We have managed out of sheer necessity." She watched him, trying to understand what he was implying, which seemed to be that they keep going like they have been for a while longer. It sounded like an awful idea to her.

"Necessity often serves as a good foundation."

"No, it doesn't, particularly not for us, Lysander. I live as a guest in your house, in a city I don't want to be in. I didn't even want to return to England. Why would we extend this further?" she exclaimed. Lysander looked taken aback. "We've been married six years——."

"Seven," Lysander interrupted.

"...and in all that time, we've shown quite clearly that we are not well-suited."

"I don't think that is true."

"I don't know what it is that gives you sentimental feelings, whether it is the idea of a child, but let's not fool ourselves—we do not belong together." Adele felt tears threaten her, prickling her eyes. It was cruel of him to suggest that they continue, and to dismiss all the hurt and rejection she felt for years on end. "Whatever it is you're feeling, it will pass; it is some kind of sentimentality that has asserted itself, but we do not fare well together." Adele turned sharply and marched away. Her tears gathering and she needed to shed them in private.

"Adele, stop," he said to her retreating back. She wasn't stopping; she needed to get back to her room and shut herself away. "I order you to stop," he said firmly.

She stopped where she was, taking a moment to calm before turning around. "You have no right exerting your authority over me." It wasn't true; he did have the right, but not the moral right.

He ran up behind her. "Adele," he said softer. "I know that I have been an awful husband."

"No, Lysander, we are awful together."

"That does not mean we cannot try to do better."

"Lysander, you almost forced yourself on me, in Adelaide." She saw shock on his face; it darkened and crumpled.

"You have not forgiven me," he said in a stark, even tone. "I have apologized for it countless times. You are unable to forgive me."

"It's not that, Lysander. I haven't forgiven you because I never felt the need. You were intent to force yourself on me and I didn't mind, because it was the only time you would touch me. In a way I was probably sorry that you stopped. That is how pathetic we are. This isn't a normal relationship and there is too much water under the bridge to pretend that it is, or even could be. For years, I wished you would acknowledge me and in my mind, it seems that I would accept anything, even force." Lysander stared at her with shock written on his features, which only went to prove her point—he had no idea how she felt. Closing her eyes, she gave a slight snort. "Let's end this now. I have tried again and again to move away from this, from all the misery that this marriage has wrought, and I do not want to be dragged back, yet again."

He didn't object this time when she walked away. Tears flowed continuously as she made her way back to the house in short, sharp strides. A passing man tried to offer her assistance, but she moved right past him. It was rude, but she couldn't deal with anyone at the moment. She knocked incessantly on the door until Jamieson let her in.

Lysander didn't return to the house. Adele wearily listened for him, but he didn't follow. Shaking her head slightly, she took a seat in front of her mirror; her face red and puffy. Whenever she managed to gain some equilibrium, he could come along and smash it. She recognized that his intentions had been well, in his mind, but he was so completely deluded—they couldn't just put their past behind them and forget about it; it didn't work that way. There was too much there—hurt, anger, resentment, to ever allow them a normal relationship as husband and wife.

Sighing as deeply as she could, she awkwardly grappled the ribbons of her corset, throwing the garment away from her onto the floor. The delusion went both ways, she admitted; she wore the damned corset so she would cut an appealing figure and there was only one person she would do that for, and it wasn't Isobel. She'd been deluding herself just as much as he, trying to continuously be presenting herself in the best light, still seeking his approval and attention. This had to end now, before they let this run further.

Chapter 28

ADELE HAD SLEPT UNEASILY that night. Their conversation in the park had run through her head all night, even in her dreams. At times, she would have regrets in how she'd responded; she could have just said yes and try to forget everything that came before, but she wasn't sure she could forgive herself in the end if it turned out to be yet another stop on this miserable journey—and chances were high that it would. Until the day before, Lysander had been adamant that he didn't want to be a husband, and with the exception of this moment of doubt, his actions had consistently proven his statement true.

Pacing around her room, she tried to settle her mind. She hadn't left the room since she'd returned the previous day, right after their confrontation in the park; she'd even dined in her room, unable to face Lysander at the moment.

Slumping down in her chair by her dresser, she wasn't sure she could be more miserable. Why couldn't he just continue being the cold, distant man and let the divorce proceed without doubt and incident? It was unfair that he should awaken some interest in this marriage now that it was in its final throes, but then everything seemed to develop a rosy sentimentality when it came to an end—even the things one never really cared for, and that was exactly the reaction Lysander was having.

It would do her no good staying here; she would be better off at Isobel's. They'd mentioned it as a good step, but they hadn't exactly agreed to mention it when Isobel had suggested it to Lysander. She'd expected his reaction to be more indifferent, but he seemed to have taken offense, and

Adele hadn't really understood why until he'd revealed that he was harboring these exuberant and irrational sentiments. His objection would have dissipated now, considering their last interaction.

The idea of being at Isobel's was appealing—escaping the tension and pressure of their interactions. Adele felt as if the past was sticking to her here, not allowing her to slip away from its grip and to turn her attention to the future. She knew what she had to do.

Waiting until Lysander returned to the house in the late afternoon, she sought him out in his study, finding him sitting in his chair, looking slightly sallow and grim. He actually looked as if he was suffering from the aftereffects of whatever it was he'd done the previous night. "I wish to visit Isobel—an extended visit," she said. "I trust you have no objections."

"Is that what you want?" he asked after a while. His eyes sought hers, seriously considering her. They were definitely back to cold and distant.

"Yes."

"Then go." He turned his attention back to his desk and ignored her.

Infuriating man, Adele thought and turned away from the study. One minute he wanted them to continue, the next he was completely indifferent, which only went to prove that his commitment to them continuing was as thin as an autumn ice layer on a pond.

Wasting no time, she packed a pair of dresses in a trunk, along with her toilette case. She didn't really need anything else—the rest could be sent for later.

*

Lysander stayed in his study, as Adele was preparing to leave. He'd made his proposition to her and she clearly wasn't interested.

Listening as she moved down the stairs, he could hear the door close and the carriage pull away. It had all happened quite quickly in the end; she was gone and he hadn't even had time to object—even if he'd been of mind to. He could have said no; he could have forced her to stay, but he wouldn't do that. If she was adamant on leaving, he wouldn't stand in her way—he'd just hoped that she had felt there was something to salvage in this marriage, but she obviously didn't. Today was the first day of his future and the previous era of his life was now over.

Silence settled on the house, the only thing to be heard was the clock on his mantle and the noise of the city outside. This was how his house always was—quiet and peaceful. It was only the last few months when it had been different, when she'd been here and strained silence hid the turmoil underneath. But now, things were returning as they should be.

He couldn't quite bring himself to wish she'd died of the cholera epidemic in India, but the drastic shifts and shocks to his life over the last year had upset his quiet, well-balanced life. That is what he needed to get back to—quiet, controlled, adult pursuits and pastimes. Adele would have a vastly different life—one she preferred—in the country, filled with nature, womanly pursuits and child-rearing. Her life would be polar opposite to his own, and she had rejected his inclusion in it, or an amalgamation of their lives.

He knew she would make an excellent mother, but he had no understanding of how he would perform as a father. From his performance as a husband, he supposed it was understandable that Adele would reject his inclusion. He couldn't help feeling bitterness at the judgment.

*

Lysander spent an indeterminable amount of time drunk. He didn't even know what time it was, the drinking

215

hall showed no indication of the state of the world outside and he could have been there for days. He'd been a frequent visitor over the last week. Harry had even sought him out here, but Lysander wasn't in the mood to talk to him; he would much rather watch the dancing girls.

"Are you planning on drinking yourself to death?"

"Just celebrating my freedom," Lysander said bitterly, his mouth awkwardly forming around the words.

"Well, I'm not sure your body is able to take much more of this celebrating. Let me take you home."

"No." Lysander didn't want to go home to his quiet house, when all he'd be doing was wishing for distraction. Sighing, Harry crossed his arms, watching the girls on stage with disinterest. "You should go home, Harry—home to your wife. She must be wondering where you are. Mine's not."

"Have you signed the petition yet?" Harry asked quietly. Lysander's tense smile faded. The petition hadn't moved since he's shoved them in that pile of documents on his desk, when Adele had come and disturbed him. He hadn't pulled it out since.

"Maybe I can have a few more drinks and you can bring it to me."

"As with any legal document, it's generally best to sign them when you're not inebriated."

"Adele wouldn't challenge me. I think she actually wants me to sign it more than you do." Silence stretched between them for a moment. "She rejected me," he said quietly.

"I'm sorry."

"Are you?" Lysander asked with a pained grimace, clearly disbelieving a word Harry was saying.

"If it truly aggrieves you, then yes, I am—but if you are upset merely because she has enough sense to want the end to this farce, then how could I be sorry?"

Lysander closed his eyes. "I know what you're saying, but why don't I feel it?"

"I don't know, Lysander. It makes no sense to me."

Sobering, Lysander stared at his friend. "If this marriage ends, I won't marry again."

"Well, if that's what bothers you, then it's a stupid statement to make."

"Adele was the perfect wife and I made a complete cockup of it." To Lysander's surprise, Harry didn't actually argue with the statement, even though he usually rushed in with a list of Adele's crimes. "And she is so giving." Lysander tried to articulate what he meant, but couldn't quite find the words. "How can someone give like that and care nothing for you?" Actually, that question rang true. He felt goose bumps travel over his skin. Now that he'd said it out loud, he knew it was the question he'd been grappling with for weeks. He looked at Harry with astonishment. "How?"

Harry sighed deeply, looking back at him. "That's not a question I can answer. But it's also not a question that one should ask when in this state," he said, indicating to Lysander's body. "My carriage is outside. Some sleep will likely do you a world of good at this point. Try philosophizing when you're sober."

Nodding slowly, Lysander watched as Harry rose, indicating for him to follow. Perhaps it was time to go home. Actually, he wanted to rush over to Isobel's house and demand an answer to his question. At least he had the question now, the one that had been preying on his mind, previously unable to form itself into cohesion.

Harry dropped him off at home and Lysander dropped heavily into the chair in his study. Throwing a glance at the clock, he saw it was after midnight. He certainly couldn't go demanding answers at this time of the night, and Harry was right—they'd never let him in the house in this state. He just hoped he'd remember the question in the morning. His eyes grew heavy and he fell asleep, knowing he would be stiff when he woke, sleeping in this position. He must be sobering up if such a concern crossed his mind.

Chapter 29

LYSANDER DID MAKE HIS WAY to his bed some time during the night and he was glad for it. It was late in the morning by the time he woke with a start, but he had a distinct mission that day. After washing, he dressed in clean clothes and prepared for the day ahead. He hadn't felt this resolute for some time. There was definitely a purpose for the day and he was going to achieve it. It was amazing how much better he felt now that he had a reason to get up in the morning.

Leaving his room, he stared at Adele's closed door, knowing most of her things were still in there, but he resisted the urge to look inside. He didn't want hints today, or to guess at her intentions; he needed answers and he wouldn't be finishing the day without them.

Again, he noticed the stark solitude of the house; it felt as if it was waiting for something. He breakfasted in the quiet dining room and read the paper, suppressing the eagerness that wanted him to skip the routines of the day. He wasn't a stickler for routine, but he wanted to wake up properly and be at his best—which admittedly, would have been helped if he hadn't gone on a mission to drink the city dry last night.

Vaguely, he remembered Harry coming and dragging him out, but he recalled none of what they talked about, except the question: how could she welcome him into her body so thoroughly if she cared nothing for him? There was an answer there—knowledge he needed; he just needed to confirm his suspicions—and it would happen today.

He didn't order his horse around, or even the carriage; he would walk, needing the space and the exercise to clear his head. He needed his wits about him for this conversation.

The day was bright and cold, and the city was fully awake by the time he made it out onto the streets. He felt anticipation running through his blood—a conclusion was drawing.

Isobel's glossy black door was closed and there was no sign of life behind the white facade. A quick knock, brought one of her footmen to the door, giving him entry. "Madam is in the salon with the little one," the man said. Lysander didn't really know Isobel's servants well, but he nodded.

"I am here to see Lady Warburton."

"She is in the parlor upstairs."

"I see."

"I will announce you."

"That won't be necessary." Lysander strode forward and up the stairs.

"Lysander," he heard Isobel calling from the salon.

"Isobel," he acknowledged and kept walking up. Isobel came running out of the salon and up the stairs, but he was quickly at the parlor, where Adele sat. She looked up at him as he entered the room, needle held over her embroidery. "I need to speak to you."

"Lysander, this is underhanded, barging in like this." Isobel came around in front of him standing between him and Adele.

"I need to speak to my wife. How can that be underhanded?"

"You could have let us know you were coming. It is not a good time."

"I recognize that you are trying to help, Isobel, but do not place yourself in my way. And this is a conversation that cannot wait. Now if you would give us a moment."

Isobel didn't look as if she was moving, so he grabbed her by the arm and walked her to the door.

"Lysander, this is my house."

"And this is my wife. Do not interfere." He placed Isobel on the other side and gave her a warning look.

"It's alright, Isobel," Adele said, smiling at his aunt. "I am sure he is not staying long."

Closing the door firmly, he turned to his wife, who was standing now, her hands wringing in front of her. "What do you want, Lysander?" she said, tension apparent in her voice.

"I want some answers." Now that he was here, he didn't know how to start this conversation.

She stood waiting, clearly not happy with this intrusion. After a while, she said, "Fine. Ask your questions."

"When you invited me into your bed—,"

"Oh please, you cannot be serious," she said, turning away.

"I am serious," he said, stepping closer, knowing it sounded ridiculous, but he had to ask this. "When you invited me into your bed, it went beyond the sheer mechanics of reproduction. You—,"

"Enjoyed it? It is sex, Lysander; it is pleasurable, even to us." She turned back to him, facing him square on.

"I am not an idiot, Adele—don't treat me like one. I know much more about sex than you do." Admittedly, she knew more than he wanted her to, particularly in regards to the other man she'd been with, but that didn't make her greatly experienced.

"Are you trying to make a point?"

"Will you let me finish." He still didn't know how to proceed. He had to change tack. "You throw this marriage away as though it means nothing, but when we were together, in your bedchamber, it wasn't absent of meaning to you."

"I never said this marriage meant nothing. It represents a great deal of pain and rejection. Lysander, please—why are you dragging this up?"

"Because this is important."

"It has never been important to you."

"I move you, deeply. Tell me it isn't true. When I touch you, you shiver. When I kiss you, you welcome it."

"What do you want from me?"

"I want you to be honest with me. Do you love me?"

She looked him in the eyes and he saw a pained expression there, but it fleeted away to resignation. "I did."

He couldn't understand her definition of love; she'd barely known him, yet she claimed that she'd loved him. But her heart had been engaged when they'd slept together; he'd felt it in his bones. "Until you met Mr. Ellingwood. Did you love him?"

*

Adele didn't exactly know what it was Lysander wanted, but it was obviously tremendously important to him at the moment. These were things better off left unsaid, but he wasn't going to let them. *Fine, we'll do this*, she said to herself and looked back at him. Did she love Mr. Ellingwood? "I cared for him and he cared for me."

"And if he hadn't died, you would be with him now." It wasn't a question, so she saw no reason to answer it. If he hadn't died, she would probably be in India now, and judging from the results of their time together, she probably wouldn't be pregnant. "What do you want from me?" he asked. "Why would you welcome me so completely if you wanted nothing from me?"

"Perhaps because I had wanted you for so very long and there were residual feelings there," she said with exasperation, trying to justify her reaction. She'd wanted him so utterly and completely those nights they'd been together.

"Residual," he repeated. "Do you love me?"

She gave him a contemptuous look. How dared he drag this all out now? "I am looking to leave all of this behind, Lysander. What purpose will this serve? Just let me go."

"Do you love me?" he repeated with more strength.

"I don't know!" she yelled back at him. "I did, and it gave me nothing but misery."

"Why would you say that you loved me when you hardly knew me?"

"Because I did. You were my husband, and I recognized you as such."

"I wanted nothing to do with you."

"That sentiment hardly escaped me."

"And then you met Mr. Ellingwood and everything changed."

"No, I realized, painfully, that things were never going to change, and then I met Mr. Ellingwood—someone who was interested in me, who thought I was a worthy person to spend time with." She saw confusion and intense concentration on his face.

"And then I dragged you back here and we developed an intimacy; one that clearly showed that there was something profound between us—one that I didn't want ended." This was unbearable. He couldn't seriously be expecting her to put up with that torture. "I don't want this marriage ended."

"I need to go, Lysander, there is too much between us."

"Too much to just let go."

"That is not what I meant."

"I love you," he said quietly.

"No, you don't," she said beseechingly. "You never did, Lysander—that is the point."

"I didn't a year ago, but I do now. I love you and you love me. Why would we end this marriage now?"

She only shook her head, feeling utterly despondent. "Lysander …"

He moved toward her quickly, bringing his hands up to her neck and pulling her to him, into a kiss, groaning into the kiss as it if released some pent up frustration. She couldn't resist the feeling of the kiss as it developed, the feelings unfurled deep inside her, compelling her and mesmerizing her. And now he knew the kind of power he still had over her.

His eyes were glassy as he pulled back from her. There was no point denying the fact that she wanted more; wanted him physically, with ferocity. For all the hurt and humiliation he'd caused her over the years, she still wanted him.

"I can force you to stay in this marriage," he said. On some level, that would make things much simpler—just removing all decisions and responsibility from her. "But I won't. If you want to be released from this marriage, I will do so. But that is not what I want. You've made me care for you—love you, and if you release me now, I will suffer exactly like I made you do."

"That's not fair."

"No, but it is true. I have the papers; you just have to ask me and I will sign them—but know this is not what I want. I want my family. I love you and I want us to be together, properly this time. If you are intent on my suffering, then you shall have it."

"I am not interested in making you suffer. That is where we've been. How would I have any assurance that I won't just be extending this misery, for both of us."

"Will my promises mean anything to you?"

She wasn't sure they would. Promises were cheap in the heat of the moment when intentions were strong; living them every day, that was hard. She shook her head and got a bitter smile in return. He didn't say anything more, just stood there for a while, watching her before turning away. He was gone before she knew what to do with herself. Her lips still burnt from the kiss and tears were spilling down her cheeks.

Isobel rushed into the room. "I love my nephew, but he is an odious man. What did he do?" she said once she'd taken a look at Adele, who was still staring after the empty space where he'd been.

An Absent Wife

Chapter 30

ADELE WALKED THE WHOLE of Hyde Park. Distress forbade her from stopping. She didn't know where she was going; she didn't know how she was feeling. Lysander's assertions reverberated through her mind. It was so incredibly unfair, making her responsible for his happiness or misery. Isobel had tried to get her to sit down and talk, but she couldn't—she needed to move, and she needed to be alone.

He'd said he loved her. Could that even be true? She knew what he was talking about when he'd said their intimacy was more than he'd expected it to be; it was for her too—scarily so. It was the reason she couldn't contemplate staying in this marriage. With intimacy and protestations of love, his ability to hurt her was so much greater.

Taking a seat on a bench, she forced herself to calm down—this distress wasn't good for the baby. Her hand stretched over her still flat stomach. He'd stated he wanted his family and Adele winced, knowing she was robbing him of that if she forced him to divorce her. Why did everything have to be so hard?

Rubbing her toe along the gravel she smiled at the irony—he was giving her everything she'd ever wanted, but at a time when she was ready to finally leave it all behind. But was she running away or was she running to; she wasn't even sure. She just wanted peace—but she wasn't going to get any if she was responsible for Lysander's misery. Or was she just scared of what he was proposing? What was she scared of? She knew the answer, but she didn't want to verbalize it.

226

She couldn't run away. Whatever her decision was to be, she had to make it with her eyes open, conscious of the consequences—otherwise, she'd never truly be happy or settled in her future.

She hated the fact that he'd left this decision all up to her. It was a tough decision and there was still an answer she was missing, and she had been honest about it—she had loved him, but did she still—even as she had been trying to put distance between them at every possible opportunity? Maybe that was proof that she did—because what would happen if she didn't maintain the distance?

*

Isobel respected her need for time and privacy, telling Adele that she was available to listen if she needed to discuss something, and reiterating what a lout her nephew was. Adele appreciated the gesture, but truthfully, she wasn't ready to talk yet.

Lying down on her bed, Adele tried to clear her mind of the jumble in there, but the demanding questions wouldn't leave her alone. His kisses melted her and he'd proven that point. Closing her eyes, she felt the touch of his lips on her; the trail of his fingers down her body—the heat inside her quickening.

She tried to imagine what it would be like to live with him as she had Samson—sleeping in the same bed, enjoying each other's bodies in calm knowledge that they were devoted to each other. She'd had stolen passion with Lysander, forbidden touches to secure this child. It was that intimacy that was causing all the trouble now—Lysander wanted more. Apparently, he'd discovered something profound and precious, and now he wasn't letting it go. She'd lied when she'd said it was just sex, because to her it had been the culmination of a decade's worth of want and need—the distant ghost made real for a few short nights.

Surely that was what he was reacting to—a sense of passion found in a rare occurrence. Rarity did not make for satisfaction over a longer period.

He'd said he loved her. That bothered her more than anything. If it wasn't true, he had no right saying it. If it was ...

She got up from the bed again, stirred by a sense of deep agitation. This would not do; she wasn't getting a moments peace. He'd come and left her with lasting torment.

Briskly, she walked to the door and down the stairs.

"Adele," Isobel called, appearing at the door of the salon as Adele was asking for her coat to be retrieved. "Where are you going?"

"I have to speak to him."

"Are you sure that is a good idea?"

"No. But it's the only thing I can do at the moment. He comes here and rips my mind and my heart into pieces, and then just leaves. That is not fair and it isn't right, and I won't let him do it to me anymore." Adele was mixing up her thoughts and speech, which probably gave Isobel a strange interpretation of what she was saying, but she couldn't worry about that right now.

Adele was out the door, greeted by the chill air, which was cooling further now that the sun was starting its descent. She marched to Lysander's house, letting her feet take her in a brisk pace down the streets, catching him as he was stepping out of his house, about to leave. "Are you going somewhere?" she demanded.

"I was, but come in." He closed the door behind them and Jamieson discreetly disappeared. "I wasn't expecting you." Stepping back, he crossed his arms in front of him as Adele paced—perhaps because he perceived that she wanted to hit him.

"I'm not responsible for you," she said.

"Yes, you are."

Adele regarded him through narrowed eyes. They'd already had this conversation, but she wasn't ready to let it go. "Look," she said. "We had some nice nights with intimacy—nice intimacy. That is not a reason to extend this marriage."

"Well, I'm in love with you now."

"No, you're not. You ignored me to close to a decade and now, at the last moment, you decided that you're in love with me. Don't you recognize how childish that seems? Why would I forgo a happy future to dabble with your emotional wobble? You've never wanted this marriage."

"I admit it. I did everything wrong. I placed you in the country and pretended you didn't exist." Adele kept pacing, then turned abruptly and hit him, repeatedly, until he'd had enough and forced her arm behind her back, bringing her to him. Adele struggled in his grip, but he wouldn't relent. "I blamed you for everything, and yes, it was unfair."

"Why should I trust you now?"

He was quiet for a moment and Adele searched his eyes, trying to understand the truth of him. "Because I'm asking you to."

"Are you just upset at losing something that you see as a possession?"

He let go of her, a look of disappointment on his face. "I was hoping you'd give me more credit than that. If that is what you think of me, then ask me to sign the petition." She stared at him, a knot of uncertainty in her chest. "If there is no future here, then just do it."

Adele felt her heart twist and her eyes tear. "I don't know what to do," she said. "If I leave, will you be fine?"

"Do you want me to lie to you?" Adele tried to pull away, but he kept her still. "I am fighting for my marriage here. What do you expect me to do?"

"Why?"

"Because we are good together. It's taken me years to realize it. Because we're having a child. Because I crave you when I'm not with you. I crave you when I am with you. Because you're all I think about."

"Your reputation will suffer if you stay with me."

"I will suffer if I don't. And so will you." His grip tightened, making her pull herself up straighter, bringing her head up to him. His eyes traveled to her lips. "I will just have to prove my steadfastness," he said. "The option is there for you. The petition is on my desk—it will stay there for you if you wish. Just give this a chance." He moved closer. Adele could feel his breath on her lips, and she closed her eyes as his lips slowly made contact with hers. True to her form, she melted into the embrace and his grip on her wrist slipped away as he deepened the kiss, instead moving to the small of her back, pressing her to him. The kiss lightened again and his tongue playfully stroked along her sensitive lips. Pulling away his eyes were drunk with desire. "Please, Adele, don't be cruel."

His eyes traveled lower along her neck, showing clearly where he wanted his mouth to be. Keeping his eyes locked on hers, his hand snaked down to the button of her jacket, and she felt it give way as he undid it, then his hand roaming over the material covering her hip. Heat unfurled deep inside her.

She didn't know whether he was manipulating her with her desire for him, but she certainly wasn't immune to it.

"This is a serious decision," she said as she tried to clear her mind of the desire that was taking over.

"Very serious," he said and leaned down, kissing her on the side of the neck.

"You're seducing me."

She could feel him smiling against the column of her neck before he resumed the kisses which threatened the stability of her knees. His hand moved higher, to cup her breast. "I love that you're not wearing a corset," he said, teasing the painfully tight bud until she moaned with exquisite delight. His other hand sought its way under her skirt and into her petticoat, until reaching the skin of her thigh.

"Lysander," she said in a breathy voice.

"Yes, my dear?" His hand moved around her bare backside, pressing her closer to him. She felt his hardness to her front.

It was meant as an objection, but now she couldn't remember why. Stepping back, he pulled her with him into his study and closed the door firmly behind them. Adele felt a glorious shock of friction as the desk stopped her backward movement, pushing her closer to his hard body. Reaching down, he lifted the material of her dress over her head, having undone the buttons at the back along the way.

As she leant back across the desk, he groaned contentedly. Her thighs coming up around him and his hands traveled along her legs, reaching her boots to undo their ties and letting them drop to the floor. Adele lay back and watched him as he finished undressing her. Her body was on fire and she couldn't stop this even if she wanted to. She wanted him inside her, deeply lodged, joining them together.

"I should have done this a long time ago," he said, his fingertips running along her bare stomach, sending sensations flowing throughout her body. Leaning in, she felt the friction of his hips to hers, but he was still dressed. She couldn't take any more of this teasing. "I'm sorry it took me so long, but I'm not letting go now. You're my wife, Adele, and you belong here with me."

By now she would agree with anything he said, but she had to admit that his words drove the heat in her, reducing her to short, sharp breaths as she waited for him. Placing her calf around his hip, she pulled him closer to her, hearing his sharp intake of breath, and brought her knees further apart in an undeniable invitation to her body.

His hips firmly lodged against hers, he undid the buttons of his waistcoat and shirt, revealing the smooth skin and firm muscles of his broad chest. Adele watched him as he undressed, feeling utterly wanton. Gone were all questions if this was the right thing, or if she trusted him— right now she didn't care; she wanted him with every base instinct in her.

Her eyes took in every detail as he undid his breeches, revealing his hardness. She really couldn't wait anymore and angled her hips to receive him, being rewarded by glorious sensations as he pushed into her, leaving her with a feeling of fullness and completion.

In all her years of imagining being with her husband, she'd never quite imagined it being quite so wanton, but she wasn't complaining—this was a new level of experience, beyond anything she'd known, and along the way, the guilt and confusion seemed to have dissipated.

A thrill of pleasure shot through her as he pushed into her completely, making her wince with the intensity of it. How could she possibly contemplate living without this? Pulling back, he pushed into her again. She couldn't breathe, but needed him more than she needed breath. Her body arched into the movement, eliciting every ounce of sensation from their coupling. Painful tension filled her as he drove her body to new heights. Powerful waves washed through her, drowning her in pleasure as he thrust into her one last time, grinding them together as if to fuse them. Sharp jerks stole through him as he shuddered through his release.

Adele wasn't sure she could move when the world started to resemble itself. Her legs felt as if they had great big weights attached, and her body was drained, too tired to move—as was her heart.

Lysander was leaning over her, breathing heavily as his lower arms took much of his weight. "I hope you don't have somewhere you need to be tonight, because that was just a prelude."

Smiling, Adele brought her arms up around his head, holding him to her chest, but a look of concern stole into her eyes. Closing her eyes, she just held him, acknowledging the beat of her rejoicing but also fearful heart. Her heart belonged to him—it always had. Being separated from him caused her pain. She was at her happiest when they were getting along, like in Venice and before, when they were here in this house, just getting along and ignoring all the difficult questions that sought to drive them apart.

"Would you really divorce me if I asked you to?"

"Well now, I know how to distract you," he said with a sly grin, leaning over and kissing her. Adele closed her eyes as the kiss contacted, sweetness stealing through her mind. She groaned in loss as he pulled away and she sighed in resignation.

More of his weight came down on her chest and he traced the curves of her brow gently with his finger. "I am asking you to give this everything. I'm asking you to trust me, and I fully acknowledge the past and all the mistakes I made. But I want us to be together, properly. Please be my wife, Adele."

Adele sat up abruptly, making him lean back and step away. "Lysander, I..." she started, pulling her dress to her to

233

cover her nakedness. Lysander looked disbelieving and hurt as he stared back at her. "I'm not sure I'm the one you want to be with. I know how you reacted to that woman at the opera. You loved her. Are you sure you're not turning your attention to me because of convenience? If she is the one you love, you should be with her."

"Nothing between us has ever been convenient, Adele. And yes, I did care for her a long time ago, when I was young, but she's not what I want. I want us. I want what we could have."

"You've hurt me so very much," she started and wrapping her arms around herself, knowing he had the power to hurt her now, more than ever.

"I know I did. I can't change the past. I would if I could. I couldn't see what was right in front of me, but I can now, and I want everything we are capable of being. Come upstairs with me," he said, moving up the staircase. Stopping, he turned and held out his hand to her. "I want you to give us a chance, to trust me, but it requires a leap of faith on your part. I'm here to catch you, but I can't do it on your behalf."

Staring at his hand which he was reaching out for her, Adele looked into his earnest eyes, feeling the years of uncertainty and misery weigh on her. She wanted to believe him with everything in her.

"Please, Adele," he said in a raw voice.

Staring at him, she couldn't believe how beautiful he was, and he was offering her everything she'd ever wanted— a desire that had burnt her so very badly. He was right; they would be miserable apart, but together they could have everything. It felt like such a great risk. But he was right; it was she who needed to take a leap of faith—faith in him. He was there, offering himself to her—she just had to accept him.

234

"I can't take any more knocks," she said. "My heart won't mend again."

"What can I say to reassure you?"

"There is nothing you can say," she said.

"Then let me show you. Every day, I will prove myself."

Out of sheer want, Adele took a step forward, feeling her heart soar, then stopped.

"And you won't bury me in the country again?"

"Not unless you take me with you."

A vision of a happy future filled her mind. She wanted it so desperately, but she could only achieve it by trusting him, and be utterly devastated if he wasn't true. Strictly, he had never lied to her, but the stakes were so very high. But then could she walk away from this—knowing what he'd proposed? The answer was no. She would be stuck in the moment forever if she did, given no peace. Both of them would suffer.

Slowly, she nodded, her insides a turmoil of fear and hope—the hope growing stronger. Taking a further step, she was at the base of the stairs. Everything she'd ever wanted stood a step up those stairs—the tender lover, the father of her child, a man who made her body sing with desire for him. And he was reaching for her.

Reaching for his hand, it was warm and assured, and there was no uncertainty in his eyes and it gave her reassurance. If she took this last step, she would live and die by its outcome. He tugged her up the stairs, where she stood a step below him, with her head at his chest. Wrapping her arms around him, she closed her eyes, feeling the solidness and warmth of his body. She just wanted to place this burden down and be with him.

Placing his hands on the sides of her head, he turned her head up to him. "I'll always catch you," he said, leaning down and kissing her softly, his lips stroking her with the gentlest of touches. A broad smile spread across his mouth. "Well then, wife, I think we need to retreat upstairs so I can give you an official welcome home. I think I need to ensure that you will never have the heart to leave again."

They didn't move for a moment, just stood there as Adele smiled up at him as his thumb stroked down her cheek and his eyes lingered, studying her face. Neither of them seemed to have the heart to break the embrace. Her husband—her beautiful husband. Suddenly it all just seemed easy, like the fear and concern had melted away. The excitement of the future filled her—their home, their child, maybe more—in a warm and loving house. Smiling again, she looked into his eyes. Lady Adele Warburton guessed she must have leapt.

Epilogue

WATCHING HIS WIFE, Lysander sat at the small mosaic table in the shaded patio of their rented house in Cairo, where they liked to hide from the midday heat. The three-story house had arched walkways facing the patio in the center of the house. They'd lived there for four months, exploring the city and the surroundings. Adele smiled as she watched her eighteen-month-old son playing with the Egyptian cook's ten-year-old daughter.

"Perhaps it's time to move on," he suggested, bringing his wife's attention to him. Reaching out for him, she let her fingers entwine with his. "Where should we go? Athens?"

"In her letter, Mrs. Callisfore said Jerusalem was marvelous."

"They both have appeal, but I think my interests are taking me more to Greece."

"Are we ready to start making our way back to England?"

"I don't know," Lysander said, looking away. "I want us to be thoroughly bonded before we go back."

Adele smiled and stroked the side of his head with her palm. "I don't think that is an issue."

"I just want your memories of us being together to be stronger than the memories from before."

"You know I don't care where we are, but saying that, I think we are ready to face the challenges of London."

Grabbing Adele's wrist, he kissed her palm. "I love you."

Adele still blushed every time he said it. "Now, Athens? How shall we travel? Timmy does adore a ship," she said, looking over at her son. "We will have to see Delphi, of course. Oh, and maybe Corinth. We could also look at going to Constantinople—wouldn't that be exciting!"

Leaning back in his chair, Lysander smiled at her exuberance. Adele loved planning travel as much as she did actually experiencing it. He would let her indulge in planning for a few weeks before he booked their passage. Their life in London could wait. It wasn't going anywhere.

To find out about new releases, please sign up to my Readers' Group at www.camilleoster.com.

Other Books by Camille Oster

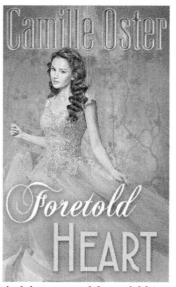

Foretold Heart - The celebrated fortune teller in Vauxhaul Garden was notoriously accurate in foretelling husbands. Or so they said. For Sylvia and her friend Ester, their prophesies were anything but comforting. Ester wasn't going to marry Marcus, whom she'd set her heart on, and for Sylvia, the prophesy pointed her in the direction of the Lord Britheney, a man with a dark history and formidable reputation. Well, fortune tellers were all charlatans, weren't they? Just a stupid act to fleece people of their coin. It was categorically not true. It just couldn't be.

The Discarded Wife – Victorian London is a cruel place for a divorcee, but with the death of Sophie Duthie's beloved second husband, she is now a widow, and independent for the first time in her life. She might not have much in terms of means, but with the help of her music shop, she can support herself and her son, Alfie. Even though her second marriage was happy, Sophie is done with husbands. Her first marriage taught her well that fairy tales are nothing more than illusions.

To Lord Aberley, his former wife is nothing but a scheming pariah, and unfortunately, his subsequent engagement wasn't successful—not that he's ever had much delusions about marriage. It is something he now wishes to avoid at all costs, but he needs an heir. It is the one duty he cannot overlook, so learning that his former wife's son is six years old, creates serious doubt about his true parentage. Seeing the child only confirms it. Alfie Duthie is his child.

The Notorious Marquis of Wickerley - With the king's execution, madness has descended on England and Cecily Alderman's father pushes forward the moment she'd been dreading for six years, her marriage to the most notorious libertine that ever graced the king's court. Sent to the wilds of Cornwall, she has to face a man exiled from all society, chased by the uncertainty and dangers of a country ripping itself apart with war. The contract to be the Marquis of Wickerley bride might be the worst injustice her father had ever visited on her, and dealing with this man who shows her no manners will prove an impossible task.

Made in the USA
Monee, IL
23 April 2021